Book Three

THE FALL OF THE HOUSE OF BLODVAT

Written by
Michael Cox

Illustrated by
Chris Smedley

*Hodder
Children's
Books*

a division of Hodder Headline Limited

The Story So Far ...

Claire and her classmate, Jason, have formed the Vampire Vigilantes – dedicated to defeating the Blodvats, vampires who are masquerading as their parents' friends, whilst secretly planning an invasion by the Undead. First, Claire's grandad is vampirised, then Jason's parents – but *everyone's* in terrible danger, especially as Hallowe'en approaches – a time when *anything* can happen!

After a hair-raising encounter with Vladimir, the Blodvats' giant vampire son, the Vigilantes find allies in Professor Weatherwax, a secret government anti-vampire agent, and in twin sisters, Poppy and Rose Mason, and their pal, Sandy. Their combined knowledge reveals that the vampire invasion is widespread, that it's been hushed up by the authorities, *and* that the worst is yet to come: a huge gathering of the Undead to mark the return of the vampire 'Master'!

Investigating further, the Vigilantes endure a terrifying onslaught by vampire bats. Then, more horror follows at Hallowe'en. After an attack on the Mason twins by the Blodvats' three monstrous daughters, Rose Mason is kidnapped and taken on board a sinister ship which begins making its way out to sea . . .

Chapter One
Well Spotted!

I n normal circumstances, the stomach-churning scream that Poppy Mason gave when she saw her terrified twin sister standing on the deck of the departing sailing ship would have drawn a crowd in no time. But these weren't normal circumstances. It was Hallowe'en.

Just minutes before, a long column of gruesome creatures had disembarked from that same sailing ship. They were now making their way up Eck Street, followed by a mob of delighted onlookers.

The crowd of revellers didn't notice Poppy's anguished cry. Nor the fact that the spectral ship was now slowly drifting away from the Chumley quayside with Rose on board. The only people taking notice of Rose's terrible predicament and Poppy's misery were the Vampire Vigilantes. And they were just as distressed as Poppy. This was the worst thing that had happened since the dreadful Blodvats had turned up in Chumley.

'The Blodvat sisters!' gasped Claire. 'Those vile vampire girls must have sneaked Rose on board.'

'My sissster!' wailed Poppy. 'They'll drink her blood! Please help meee! I don't know what to do to save her!'

'Don't worry, Poppy,' said Claire, trying to remain calm. 'We'll think of something.'

'Surely there must be some way we can rescue her!' cried Sandy.

'But – but—' cried Darren, jumping around like a cat on a hot tin roof.

'Oh, do be quiet, Darren!' Claire said irritably. 'Don't you think you've done enough damage for one evening by just standing and watching when you first saw the twins being kidnapped?' Then she saw Darren's face crumple. 'Oh Darren!' she cried. 'I'm sorry, I didn't mean that. What is it you want to tell us?'

'Those three awful vampire girls who kidnapped Poppy and her sister aren't actually on that ship!' said Darren. 'They're over there on the quayside. Next to that stack of boxes.'

5

'In that case,' cried Jason, 'who's on the boat with Rose?'

As he spoke, a large figure boogied wildly across the ship's deck. It was Vladimir, the Blodvat sisters' gigantic vampire brother. In addition to his 'Scariest Spook in Chumley' sash, he was now wearing Rose's Discman and snapping his fingers frantically. Spotting his stranded sisters, he waved at them cheerfully.

'Vladimir!' gasped Jason. 'He must have pulled a fast one on the three stick insects and got Rose away from them! Look! They're absolutely livid!'

All three were now jumping up and down on the edge of the quayside and frenziedly shaking their fists as they mouthed silent threats and curses.

'But why don't they just fly across?' said Sandy. 'After all, they are ubervampires!'

'Too risky,' said Claire. 'If they were spotted it would blow their cover completely.'

At that moment one of the sisters let out a scream, followed by a big splash. Diptheria had lost her footing on the slippery stonework. She thrashed wildly around in the freezing Eck, gasping for breath and spitting out great mouthfuls of water. Vladimir was now watching his sister's watery struggles with obvious pleasure.

'Let's hope she's wearing her concrete undies!' said Jason.

'Can the Undead swim?' asked Sandy.

'I'm not sure,' said Claire, as she watched Scrofula and Bacteria dash down the quayside steps and attempt to pull their struggling sister from the river. 'But I think Rose is going to be quite safe from those three for the time being.'

'What about *him*?' cried Poppy. 'What will he do to Rose?'

'From the look of things,' said Claire, 'the worst that's likely to happen is that he'll ask her for a bop! But she isn't out of danger. He *is* a vampire, after all. If only there was some way we could get to them.'

'I'm a brilliant swimmer,' said Darren. 'I could try swimming across and rescuing her.'

'Don't be crazy, Darren,' said Claire. 'Those currents are treacherous. And there's a sea mist coming in. That would make it twice as dangerous.'

'Anyway,' said Sandy. 'They'll be round the big bend soon. You'd never catch them!'

'I've a better idea,' said Jason. 'The river twists and turns before it leaves town. If we cut back up Eck Street then cross the market place we can probably reach the big bridge on Whitby Road before the ship does.'

'Good idea!' said Claire. 'We'll have to be really fast, though. That ship can move like the wind!'

'But what will we do when we get there?' said Sandy.

'We'll cross that bridge when we come to it!' said Jason.

'Do you think the sisters spotted us?' said Sandy, as they hurried up Eck Street.

'They didn't,' said Darren. 'They were busy hauling the beanpole out of the water.'

'Well, that's something,' said Claire. 'The last thing we want is those monstrosities following us. We've got enough problems as it is, like making our way through this lot. Can you believe the size of this crowd?'

A seething mass of Hallowe'eners was completely blocking their way.

'Cripes!' said Jason. 'Where did they come from? There's squillions of them!'

'That horrendous bunch of ghouls from the ship have got mixed up with the Spook Parade,' said Sandy. 'And the way this fog's coming down you soon won't be able to tell which one's which!'

The Vigilantes were suddenly alerted by a cry of terror. Across the street, partially hidden by the ever-thickening mist, a chubby man was cowering in front of two tall, cloaked and hooded vampires. As one of them seized him by his collar the man put up his hands to defend himself, then cried, 'Please don't harm me! I'm a doctor. The people in this town need me!'

'It's Dr Grainger!' gasped Jason. 'It looks

9

like he's in trouble!'

'*Now* what do we do?' groaned Claire.

Before the Vigilantes could do anything, Dr Grainger let out a burst of his famous *infectious* laughter. He grinned up at his attackers and said, 'Now here's a good one. What's a vampire's favourite soup? Scream of mushroom! Ha ha ha. And you'll love this one. What do you call a vampire centre forward? A ghoul scorer! Ha ha ha!'

'Hmmph!' said Sandy, as the Vigilantes breathed a sigh of relief. 'False alarm!'

'Definitely!' said Jason. 'If he's cracking jokes, he's bound to be OK!'

'I hope so!' said Claire, as they set off again. 'Because we haven't time to stop. It's Rose who needs our help!'

A few moments later they were just beginning to fight their way through the scrum when Claire saw her mum and dad, talking to Sergeant Watt. Before Claire could disappear into the crowd her mum beckoned her over.

'Claire!' said her mum. 'Enjoying yourself? It's turning out to be quite a night, isn't it, with these extra ghouls and that fabulous ghost ship? Did you see it?'

'Err, yes, I did,' said Claire. Then she looked at her watch and said, 'What was it you wanted, Mum?'

'Sergeant Watt was just asking if we'd seen anything of the skateboard thief. Apparently he's been up to all sorts of mischief!'

'It's serious,' said Sergeant Watt. 'There's no telling where that maniac will strike next. I've got my men combing the town for him. Our last reported sighting was down at Eck Wharf. If you do see him get to a phone immediately!'

'I will,' said Claire. 'But I've got to go now. My pals are waiting.' Then she paused and said, 'By the way, I thought you were supposed to be with Bruno and Hildegard. Where are they?'

'We lost them,' said her dad. 'The last time we saw them they were talking to Mr Legg. And you know what the Blodvats are like once they get nattering. They could chew the hind leg off a donkey!'

Or the neck off a greengrocer, thought Claire.

Claire caught up with the other Vigilantes

as they were breaking through the far edge of the crowd. Six minutes later they reached the Whitby Road and began sprinting for the bridge. Claire dashed to the centre and immediately looked back up the mist-shrouded river in the direction of Eck Wharf. Then she gave a sigh of relief. There was no sign of the ship. 'Brilliant!' she cried. 'We got here before it!'

'No we didn't,' said Jason. '*It* got here before *us*!'

Claire turned and saw that Jason was looking downriver. Silhouetted in the murk, about sixty metres away and rapidly making its way towards the open sea, was the spectral sailing ship.

'Oh no!' cried Sandy. 'We've missed it!'

Poppy burst into tears. 'We've lost my sister!' she cried. 'I'll never see her again. She's gone for ever!'

A feeling of utter gloom and despair descended on the Vigilantes. After their mad dash along the Whitby Road all they could manage to do was lean on the bridge's stone parapet and stare hopelessly down into the swirling mist below them.

'I know we're supposed to be on

undercover work for the Professor but we're just going to have to go to the police,' said Sandy. 'This really is serious!'

As he spoke a police-car siren began to wail somewhere in the distance.

'Sounds like they're on their way already,' said Darren.

'Listen!' said Jason. 'What's that?'

'A police car!' said Darren. 'I've just told you!'

'No, not that!' said Jason. 'It's something else. Much quieter and nearer. Listen!'

The Vigilantes stood very still. Then they heard it. It was a gentle *plash plash plash,* coming from somewhere beneath them. They leaned over the parapet as far as they dared and peered down, but at that moment the mist thickened so that it was difficult to see anything. However, they continued to stare and a few seconds later the mist swirled and cleared slightly, giving them a view of the river.

A small rowing boat was emerging from beneath the bridge. It turned and began to head towards the riverbank. It contained one large figure and one small one. The large one was rowing slowly and steadily while the small one sat hunched on the boat's rear seat.

'It's *them*!' hissed Claire, hardly able to contain her excitement and relief.

'Brilliant!' whispered Jason. 'Vladimir's brought her back.'

'Let's hope so,' said Claire, then she looked at Poppy. She seemed to be on the verge of crying out to her sister so Claire gently tapped her arm and made a sign for her to be quiet. The last thing they wanted was for Vladimir to take fright.

The boat reached the shallow water at the river's edge and Vladimir drew in the oars. He climbed out and pulled the boat on to the bank. Then he beckoned for Rose to get out too. Looking dazed, but otherwise unharmed, she scrambled up the bank. Vladimir gave her a big fangy grin and took off her Discman. As he held it out and she reached to take it, he opened his mouth to speak. But his words remained frozen on his lips.

At that moment a uniformed figure loomed up out of the gloom on the riverside path and a deep voice boomed, 'Oh no you don't, my lad! Looks like we've caught you red-handed. So, it's personal stereos this time!'

At the same instant, the police siren suddenly became quite deafening and a patrol car whizzed past and screeched to a halt a little further along the bridge.

Sergeant Watt leapt out, dashed to the long flight of steps that led to the riverside, then began bounding down them two at a time.

'Keep him there! I'll be with you in two ticks!' he yelled to the policeman who'd just shouted at Vladimir. 'And here come reinforcements!'

A third policeman was charging along the riverside path from the direction of Eck Wharf.

'Got you!' he said. 'No way are you getting away this time, my lad!' Then he looked at Rose and said, 'Step away please, miss. This might get a bit lively!'

Clutching her Discman and still looking like she was in some sort of topsy-turvy dream, Rose stepped back, out of harm's way.

'Right, boys!' yelled Sergeant Watt. 'Let's have him!' With that, he and his two constables rushed at Vladimir.

And then the mist closed in again.

The Vigilantes weren't entirely sure what happened next. There was a lot of scuffling and yelling and at one point they definitely heard one of the policemen shout, 'Got you, you ruffian! Let's have that mask off now!' Then they heard Sergeant Watt yell, 'That's my blooming face you've just tried to pull off!' A moment later there was a splash and another voice said, 'You blithering idiot! You've just pushed me in the bloomin' Eck!'

After a few more minutes of noisy chaos they finally heard Sergeant Watt cry, ''S all right, lads, I've got him this time!' and then, in a rather less confident voice, he added, 'At least, I think I have!'

When the mist cleared, a rather amazing

scene met the Vigilantes' eyes. One of the constables was sitting on the riverbank emptying water from his boot; the other was handcuffed to the railings next to the bridge, and Sergeant Watt was stretched full-length on the riverside path desperately clinging to the back leg of an enormous Dalmatian puppy, which was frantically twisting and turning as it tried to free itself from his grasp.

'What the—' cried Sergeant Watt, when he saw what he'd bagged. 'Where the 'eck did that come from?'

'It's a dog!' said one of the constables.

'Well spotted!' cried Sergeant Watt.

'*Really* well spotted!' said the policeman. 'It's a flippin' Dalmatian!'

'Less of the wisecracks,' yelled Sergeant Watt. 'What I want to know is where that yobbo's got to. This is no time for jokes and leg pulling!'

Then he noticed that he was still hanging on to the dog's leg, so he quickly let go of it. A microsecond later the Dalmatian was bounding up the steps towards the Whitby Road. Halfway up the steps it met the Vigilantes who were now on their way down. As it brushed past Claire she saw that tangled around its neck were some tattered remnants of pink satin sash on which she could just make out the words 'Chumley' and 'Spook'.

'Vladimir!' she gasped.

The dog stopped in its tracks, looked up at her, wagged its tail furiously, then bounded on. Moments later it reached the top of the steps and disappeared from sight.

Sergeant Watt was now on his feet, brushing the mud from his uniform. 'Just our luck!' he moaned. 'We had him! Then that dopey great dog had to turn up and spoil things.' Then he turned to Rose and said, 'Well, miss, at least you've still got your little record player. Didn't harm you, did he?'

Almost too stunned to speak, Rose shook her head and said, 'Err – no.'

'Well, that's good,' said Sergeant Watt. Then he looked stern. 'Now, you really shouldn't be wandering along lonely riverside paths at this time of night. We'll take you home in the squad car!'

'It's all right, Sergeant!' said Rose, spotting the Vigilantes. 'My friends are here now. I'll go with them.'

'Yes!' said Claire. 'We'll look after her.'

'We'll leave her with you, then,' said

18

Sergeant Watt. He turned to his constables, 'OK lads. Let's get after him!'

'Err, before we do,' said the handcuffed constable, 'could I ask a favour?'

'What?' said Sergeant Watt.

'Unlock me from these railings!'

'You better, Sarge!' said the other policeman. 'You don't want him taking a fence!'

Chapter Two
The Dust of Dracula

As the Vigilantes made their way back towards the centre of Chumley, Rose told them how the sisters had let go of her for a moment when they'd got really excited about the arrival of the spooky sailing ship, and how she'd taken the opportunity to slip away, only to be caught by Vladimir a few minutes later.

'He didn't seem to want to hurt me,' said Rose. 'He just kept pointing at my Discman and grinning. So I gave it to him and showed him how to put the CDs on. Then he hid me from the girls and the minute he saw his chance he smuggled me on board the ship. I think rescuing me was probably his way of saying thank you for the Discman.'

'What was it like on the ship?' said Claire.

'Weird!' said Rose. 'Freezing cold and really

spooky. I never saw any sailors or anything, but I'm sure there must have been some. Anyway, as soon as we were out of sight of the wharf Vladimir lowered that little boat and we climbed down to it. Then he started slowly rowing us down the river until he saw a good place to stop. And that's when you saw us!'

'Did he speak to you, Rose?' said Claire.

'Not at first. But when he was rowing, he tried to sing along with my Discman. Even though I was terrified I couldn't help smiling and that sort of broke the ice. A moment later he began talking and once he got going there was no stopping him.

'First he told me he hated being a vampire. And hated drinking blood and sometimes even fainted at the sight of it. Then he told me he was really good at skateboarding and dancing and wanted to be a human "Perishable" like me and have lots of "Perishable" friends. But after that he looked really sad and said he knew he couldn't really because deep down he was a vampire and had to help make lots of Dracmares and find out where the Master was, because that's what they'd come to England for.'

'Cripes!' said Claire. 'And here's us thinking

this Master would be coming here from Tonsilveinia or wherever. But now it sounds like he's been here all the time. And that they don't know *where* he is.'

'Wait till I tell you the next bit,' said Rose. 'Vladimir said that the Master had been turned to dust a long time ago when some bad English Perishables had stuck their big knives into him. The Perishables had put the dust in a little box and brought it to England and hidden it from all the other vampires in the world. And he said that when Bruno and Hildegard find the box, they're going to make the Master undead. They've got a big black coach and horses all ready for him. When all the other vampires see the Master riding in the coach they'll all love the Blodvats, because they will have brought back the King of the Vampires!'

'If I had a little light bulb stuck on top of my head right now, I think it would have just lit up!' said Claire. 'Remember I told you that Professor Weatherwax gave me the story of Count Dracula to read? Well, that business with knives and the English Perishables is exactly what happens at the end of the book. The friends from England, led by this Jonathan Harker, chase Count Dracula across

Europe. Then, just before he gets to his castle, they catch him and stick their knives in him and he turns to dust.'

'Are you trying to say that the Blodvats might believe the Dracula story is true?' said Sandy. 'And they're looking for his remains?'

'Why not?' said Claire. 'Who knows how they think? And what about all those people who watch soaps on TV and believe the characters are real and send them birthday cards and stuff? And they're just telly addicts, not crazy vampires!'

'But how do they actually turn a destroyed vampire back into an all-biting, all-sucking Undead?' asked Sandy.

'I know!' said Poppy. 'They pour the blood of the person who did the destroying over the vampire's remains. Or failing that, the blood of the vampire slayer's descendant!'

'*Harker!*' exclaimed Claire. 'That's it! Jonathan Harker's the one who struck the fatal blow in *Dracula*. The Blodvats must think my grandpa, Reg Harker, is one of his descendants! That's why they've been trying to vampirize him all this time – as well as using him to find hidey holes for their undead pals, and trying to steal his blood pudding

23

recipes. They must have been draining his blood, ready to pour over the dust of the Master!'

'Cripes, Claire,' said Sandy. 'It fits! I think you've got it!'

'There's one bit I don't understand,' said Claire. *Dracula* ends when the Count crumbles to dust. There's no mention of Jonathan Harker and his mates putting the dust in a box and bringing it to England.' She turned to Rose and said, 'Did Vladimir tell you anything else?'

'Not much more,' said Rose, 'but he did say that someone called Wolfgang knew where the box was and was helping them to look for it. He said that Bruno and Hildegard are getting really angry with Wolfgang because even though he knows where it is he's taking too long to find it. Then we arrived at the big bridge, so that was that.'

'Rose,' exclaimed Claire, 'you've been brilliant! Because of you we know absolutely loads about what the Blodvats are up to.'

The whole time the Vigilantes had been listening to Rose, Darren had remained silent, with his eyes as wide as saucers and his jaw drooping like a pair of baggy underpants. Now he finally spoke up.

'About an hour ago I was wandering around Chumley, enjoying some innocent Hallowe'en fun. Before I knew what was happening, I got mixed up with a real vampire kidnapping. I saw loads of vampire spooks get off some sort of ghost ship, and I ended up chasing a giant vampire boy who somehow managed to turn himself into massive great spotty dog! And now I've just been listening to you lot going on about "Perishables" and the dust of Dracula. I really do need someone to tell me what's happening.'

Over the next fifteen minutes the Vigilantes told him the whole story of Bruno and Hildegard Blodvat, and their astonishing vampire children. Darren's mouth opened even wider when they told him how they'd formed themselves into an anti-vampire group and were working with a top government agent, called Professor Wilton Weatherwax, in an effort to defeat the horrendous undead hordes which had recently invaded Britain.

When Claire finally asked him if he wanted to join the Vampire Vigilantes, he nodded so enthusiastically that it looked like his head would fall off and bounce along the

25

pavement. Then, agreeing to meet soon to try and make even more sense of all the stuff about the hidden remains of the 'Master', the exhausted Vigilantes all made their way home.

The moment Claire got in, she went straight to her grandpa's room. To her dismay, not only did he have even more sinister red marks on his neck (the ones her parents believed were razor nicks), but his eyes now seemed to be glowing a very weird shade of pink.

When she asked if Hildegard and Bruno had called, he pulled his bedcovers over his head and mumbled something about wanting to be left alone. Claire decided it would be pointless (and possibly dangerous) to question him further, so she went to her own room.

Once there, she sent off a long e-mail to Professor Weatherwax relating every single detail of all that the Vigilantes had seen and heard during Hallowe'en night in Chumley. Then she crawled into bed and was soon fast asleep, dreaming of boogying vampires, laughing policeman, giant Dalmatians, and the dust of Dracula.

Chapter Three

Missing!

The next morning the talk in Chumley was of nothing but Fright Night and what a tremendous success it had been.

The hit of the evening had been that spectacular stunt with the spoof spectral sailing ship and the professional actors who'd carried their coffins up Eck Street, then so mysteriously vanished as the fog came down. No one was entirely sure who had put on this amazing bit of street theatre but everyone agreed that it was Chumley's best Fright Night ever.

Later that same day, the mood in the town suddenly changed to utter gloom when it was discovered that two much-loved and well-respected Chumleyites were missing. One was Mr Legg and the other was Dr Grainger.

The moment Claire heard about the

shocking disappearances she immediately recalled the two hooded figures that had been menacing Dr Grainger. She also remembered what her dad had said about the Blodvats chatting with Mr Legg and guessed that Bruno and Hildegard had been interested in far more than just his carrots and cauliflowers!

Her first thought was to go to the police but the Professor had said it was vital not to involve outside forces. She decided to send another e-mail to the Professor and switched on her computer, only to find that she already had an e-mail waiting for her.

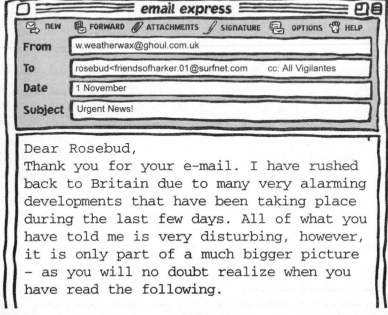

email express

NEW   FORWARD   ATTACHMENTS   SIGNATURE   OPTIONS   HELP

From w.weatherwax@ghoul.com.uk

To rosebud<friendsofharker.01@surfnet.com   cc: All Vigilantes

Date 1 November

Subject Urgent News!

Dear Rosebud,
Thank you for your e-mail. I have rushed back to Britain due to many very alarming developments that have been taking place during the last few days. All of what you have told me is very disturbing, however, it is only part of a much bigger picture – as you will no doubt realize when you have read the following.

28

1) The arrival of that ship and its loathsome cargo signals that the Undead have now begun the final and most dangerous phase of their operation.

2) The Undead often find it impossible to distinguish fact and fiction. The Blodvats' search for the remains of Count Dracula would be almost laughable if it wasn't so deadly serious.

3) There has been a massive exodus of the Undead from London – large numbers of bats leaving the Underground system and flying north overnight.

4) During the week leading up to Hallowe'en, disappearances occurred throughout the North. One hundred and fifty people are now missing from towns and villages in Yorkshire alone.

5) We have had reports of several sightings of Mr Pither. It would also appear that he is not staying with relatives in Moulton. His aunt says she has not heard from him in weeks and is getting quite worried.

It is most urgent that I meet you and the other Vigilantes. There is an abandoned warehouse that stands by the Eck on the Eckford Road about half a mile out of Chumley. I will be there at 4.15 pm the day after tomorrow. It is vital that you meet me!

Best wishes, Professor Weatherwax

On Thursday afternoon, clad in coats and carrying torches, the Vigilantes gathered at the warehouse. As they anxiously discussed the disappearances, they heard a vehicle draw up outside. A moment later, the Professor came in, looking worried and exhausted. After introducing him to the newest recruits, Claire offered him a wooden box to sit on, while the Vigilantes perched themselves on some old straw bales.

'First, I would like to thank you for all you have done so far,' said the Professor. '*And* give a special word of thanks to Rose. Finding out about the Blodvats' misguided quest for the remains of the Master was a real scoop! But more on that later, because I have much to tell *you*. As you will now know, the Undead have all left London, and the other places they were lurking.'

'Where are they *now*?' said Poppy.

Professor Weatherwax took a breath, then said, 'Here in Chumley and the surrounding Eck Valley – in the caves and potholes that honeycomb the hills and moors, and remote graveyards and long-forgotten burial sites. And it wouldn't surprise me if some were tucked away in the sewers. They've been coming for

days. You witnessed the arrival of one ghastly group on Hallowe'en night. However, huge numbers of others will have come more stealthily, and entirely undetected.'

'But what are they all doing?' said Jason.

'At the moment they're lying low,' said the Professor. 'Some, like the Blodvats, will be mingling with the locals, passing themselves off as tourists and business people. They will be responsible for co-ordinating the final stages of their odious operation. Others will have gone to ground.' He looked at Jason. 'In fact, they will be snuggled down in those err – building materials that your father's lorry fleet has been transporting from the docks at Hartlepool. Or the "good earth of home", as the Undead prefer to think of it.'

'But won't all these hundreds of vampires need to feed?' said Claire. 'They're going to need an awful lot of blood, aren't they?'

The Professor suddenly looked very serious. 'It would seem that they are deliberately going through some sort of fasting – almost as if they are preparing themselves for some great orgy of guzzling.'

'But what about all those people that have disappeared?' said Poppy. 'Won't they be attacking them?'

'I was coming to them,' said Professor Weatherwax. 'But before I do, I'd like to ask if you know what is meant by blood groups?'

'I do,' said Sandy. 'My mum works at Eck Valley General and I've heard her talking about them. We've all got different sorts, haven't we?'

'That's right,' said Professor Weatherwax. 'Different people have different types of blood which are given names like B-positive or A-negative.

'Now, in some way that my scientists and I have yet to fathom, all vampires have a heightened sensitivity. If a vampire were to pass you in the street, it would be able to identify your blood group, simply by sniffing the air you breathed out. And, of course, if yours was a blood type that interested it, it would immediately mark you out for future attention – if you know what I mean.'

'Yikes!' said Claire. 'That's scary!'

'Yes,' said the Professor. '*Very* scary! And for vampires, these blood groups are incredibly exciting. For example, type B-positive would be a fizzy, fruity drink to enjoy on a summer's evening. While blood type A-positive is an everyday kind of drink, like tea or cocoa. And blood type B-negative is revolting to all vampires – a mixture of cough medicine and vinegar! However, there is one blood type that all vampires consider to be the most desirable of all. One swig and they are dancing on air. Soon the powerful blood proteins kick in. Most undead would do anything to be able to drink this particular sort of blood.'

'Which type is it?' said Claire.

'It's type AB-negative,' said the Professor. 'The rarest of blood types. Only one person in every hundred has this sort. When I heard of all those people going missing I got my agents to run some checks on the folk who had vanished. Every single one of them has blood type AB-negative!

'It would seem that the Blodvats are amassing a huge stockpile of AB-negative blood. A human has four-and-a-half litres in their body. At last count, at least three hundred people had disappeared from the North of England. So the Blodvats and their accomplices now have more than thirteen hundred litres of very special blood on tap! And don't forget that for a vampire, only one swig is needed to achieve that magic AB-negative moment. So there's enough blood for very big vampire party indeed!'

Darren suddenly looked horrified and said, 'So have the vampires drained all the blood out of these people's bodies, just so they can have a big party?'

'Oh no!' said Professor Weatherwax. 'They won't have drained them, not yet. That would be like killing the geese that the lay golden eggs. They will simply be siphoning off their blood a few litres at a time!'

'Like Dad and Mum milk our herd of dairy cows,' said Poppy.

'Exactly!' said the Professor. 'And like

cattle, they will no doubt have those poor people penned up. The Blodvats and their horrendous helpers will soon be turning this excellent red liquid into premium grade human blood sausages. Which they are no doubt planning to sell to the verminous hordes who are gathered in the Eck Valley!'

'And they'll be using my Grandpa Reg's black-pudding-making equipment!' exclaimed Claire. 'No wonder Bruno was all excited about making lots of Dracmares!'

'Yes,' said the Professor. 'Making enormous amounts of money is undoubtedly one of the main reasons they are here. Living in a huge castle in Tonsilveinia and driving a big car doesn't come cheap. The Blodvats are not just ubervampires. They are also ruthless business vampires!'

'So is that what they've come to Chumley for,' said Rose. 'To have a big party and make lots of money?'

'No,' said Professor Weatherwax. 'There is another purpose. And it involves those dusty remains of the "Master". As far as the Blodvats are concerned, one of the high points of this whole event will be the resurrection of Count Dracula. It would be the perfect accompaniment to the launch of their sickening new sausage product.'

'But those remains don't exist,' said Claire.

Professor Weatherwax chuckled. 'We know that! But barmy Bruno and horrendous Hildegard don't. It would appear that they firmly believe the remains are here. So why should we disappoint them? The last thing we'd want is them abandoning their little event. I think we should definitely make sure they find what they're looking for.'

'What?' said Sandy. 'Like plant a box with some some pretend remains in it?'

'Exactly!' said the Professor. 'We might even arrange for the "Master" himself to put in an appearance. However, I am getting carried away. We have more serious matters to discuss, like this event itself. On this occasion the Undead hordes will be doing something that happens once every hundred years.'

'What?' said Darren.

'Huge numbers of them will be gathered in one place!' replied the Professor. 'It will present a golden opportunity for my team and our Extreme Exterminator forces to strike a massive blow against them. But, if we miss it, all will be lost. When it is over the Undead will disperse, refreshed and rejuvenated. They will once again infiltrate society and wreak havoc.

'It is vital we discover what this event will involve, and when it will take place and where. Today is the third of November. Unless they are in one of their extended sleeps, the Undead can only go without blood for a very short time. Whatever is planned will take place in the next few days.'

'But that gives us hardly any time at all!' said Sandy.

'Exactly!' said the Professor. 'I am relying on you to help me in my search for clues. I personally have just a few more leads to follow. One of them is the government Minister for Tourism, Sir Norman Goreman. At the beginning of the year Sir Norman and a dozen of his closest aides paid an official visit to Tonsilveinia. During their stay they spent several days at Castle Blodvat. I suspect that during that time they were—'

'Turned into vampires?' said Jason.

'I fear so!' said the Professor. 'One of my spies in Sir Norman's department tells me that he and his colleagues have been eating some very unusual lunches lately. Raw liver sandwiches, uncooked quarter pounders, huge bloody steaks eaten straight from the bone. And there was recently a rumour about an incident involving Sir Norman's teeth and the neck of the rather plump workman who had come to install his new telephone system.

'But I have no concrete proof of any of these things. What I do know is that it was he who pulled strings within the government and arranged for the Blodvats to visit your school, and for them to be introduced to Mr Pither. I have a meeting booked with Sir Norman and some of his people this evening. I will be asking him about his Tonsilveinian trip. And why his friends, the Blodvats, so desperately wanted to speak to your teacher. And that is why I must soon leave you!'

'Talking of Mr Pither,' said Claire, 'have you found out anything else?'

'Yes,' said the Professor. 'It would appear that when he is not teaching or twitching, your teacher leads another life!'

'Cripes!' said Claire. 'He's not a secret vampire, is he?'

'No, nothing so sinister!' laughed the Professor. 'But he *is* an expert on the Undead, particularly on films and books about them, like *Dracula*. He does guided Dracula walks

38

around Whitby during the school holidays, showing tourists all the places that are mentioned in the book. And we also believe that he is something of a budding horror writer. But we have yet to see any of his work.'

The Professor looked at his watch then said, 'Now, I really must be going. I will return to Chumley as soon as I've seen Sir Norman. And then, Vigilantes, we will all work as one big team! We will arrange for the beastly Blodvats to discover that box of dust they desire so desperately. I'll get my special effects chaps to come up with something suitably convincing. In the meantime, put your heads together and think hard. Please, leave no stone unturned!'

Chapter Four

Vampire Bytes

Next day, all the schools in the Eck Valley were closed for teacher training, so the Vigilantes got together at Jason's house. It also happened to be the day before Bonfire Night. However, the Vigilantes had far more important things to think about.

'There must be something we can do,' said Claire. 'Jason, what about your idea of looking for a real vamp website with that snazzy bit of Internet software you dreamed up? Haven't you had any luck?'

'The best thing was finding the Professor,' said Jason. 'I haven't got anywhere since then. I must have banged in ten zillion different address combinations and come up with zilch! Look – I'll show you!'

He clicked his cursor arrow on the 'Random Search' icon. A moment later a browser window opened, his 'Internet Connected' symbol began to flash and the words 'Undead World' appeared in the location box.

'Here it goes again,' said Jason, pointing to the message which had just appeared:

The specified server could not be found.
The specified server could not be found.

'I hate to think how many times I've seen that blinking message. And when I do get a hit, it's nothing that might be linked to the Blodvats.' Then he paused and said, 'Blood. Blood Dungeon. Blood Suckers. Neck suck. Night. Nightflier. Bat. Batbites. I've tried them all!'

'What about "fang"?' said Poppy. 'Vampire? Nosferatu? Grave news? Blodvat.com?'

'Tried the lot!' said Jason.

Darren said, 'What about "vampire bites"? I mean, that is what they give you, isn't it?'

'Hmmm, very inspired!' said Jason a bit sarcastically, then quickly added, 'Oh, go on then, Darren, give it a bash. I've probably already tried it but it might be worth a go.'

Darren nodded enthusiastically, then slowly typed, http://www.vampirebytes.com

Claire was the first to spot his mistake. 'Oh, Darren,' she cried, 'you don't spell that sort of bites like that. The second letter's an "i" not a "y"!'

But by then he'd clicked the 'Open Location' box. And rather than displaying the 'Server could not be found' message that had frustrated Jason so many times, the on-screen display quickly moved through a series of search status messages. A second later it said: 'Connecting to http://www.vampirebytes.com.'

'You've scored a hit!' said Sandy.

'Yes,' said Jason, rather more cautiously. 'But let's not get too excited. It might be more vampire twaddle!'

'Look!' said Claire. 'A page is building. Let's watch and see what happens.'

Pixel by pixel, block by block, two familiar faces were beginning to take shape in the middle of the screen.

'I don't believe it!' gasped Jason. 'It can't be!'

'Yes it is!' cried Claire. 'It's them!'

Staring out from Jason's computer screen were the smiling faces of Hildegard and Bruno Blodvat!

'Wow!' cried Sandy, turning to Darren and slapping him on the shoulder. 'You're a little genius. Well done, Darren!'

'This is fantastic!' said Poppy. 'Quick! Let's get into the site before it crashes or disappears.'

The page was completely formed now and beneath the Blodvats' faces was a door icon. Jason clicked on it and, as a new display appeared, the Vigilantes all groaned.

'Oh no!' said Jason as a whole page of completely unreadable script appeared. 'It's all in Tonsilveinian. Just like Bruno's notebook!'

'Stay calm,' said Claire. 'This is a world wide website.' She pointed to a row of flags in the corner of the screen. Jason clicked on the British one and a new page, entirely in English, entitled 'Vampire Bytes', began to take shape. The Vigilantes had really and truly reached the home page of Bruno and Hildegard Blodvat: ubervampires, web vampires, and rampant business vampires!

A huge menu stretched from top to bottom. Today's offering was 'Once bitten, twice dry', by a

vampire calling himself Flesh Gored-On. There was a travel page called the 'Around the World in Eighty Slurps', and a news page entitled the 'Infernal Journal'. There was so much to see that the Vigilantes didn't know where to go first. In the end Jason clicked at random. The link he chose immediately took them to a page plastered with ads for dozens of products and services, every one of which seemed to have something to do with Bruno and Hildegard Blodvat.

'Look at this one,' cried Rose. '"To rent: one crypt – oodles of really bad atmosphere – cold running slime. Apply to Castle Blodvat, Tonsilveinia."'

'And this!' said Poppy. '"Undead – but unwed? Maybe we can help! One hundred and twenty-year-old; own teeth; would like to meet similar – with view to evenings out. For hundreds more like this follow the text links to Blodmates!".'

'And what about this?' said Sandy. '"Rest in peace. Chill out in a 'Blodbox'! The ultimate in luxury coffins. Air de-conditioning. Central locking. Electric lid. Test sleeps and part exchange deals available." The Professor was right! They really are a couple of business enterprise vampires, aren't they?'

'Not half!' said Poppy. 'There's so much to see, I could spend all day surfing this!'

'Don't you think we're getting a bit carried away?' said Jason. 'I know this is incredibly interesting but we're forgetting what we're supposed to be looking for.'

'You're right,' said Claire. 'Time's precious. We must focus. Try that events link.'

As Jason clicked on it, a bouncing skull appeared in the centre of the screen. Above it were the words:

| VERY IMPORTANT ANNOUNCEMENT |
| ALL UNDEAD: CLICK HERE NOW! |

Jason clicked on the bouncy skull and a new page immediately began to build. In three more seconds it was up and done and the Vigilantes immediately knew they'd found what they were looking for!

45

Blood brothers and sisters everywhere, your hosts,
Dr Bruno and Madam Hildegard Blodvat,
cordially invite you to the Evilent of the Century!

THE GREAT REVIVAL,
THE RETURN OF THE MASTER

and the launch of *THE BLODFURTER*

*PERISHABLE JUICE LIKE YOU'VE NEVER
TASTED IT BEFORE!*

(free sample for every vampire attending!)

ALL TO BE ACCOMPANIED BY:

• Oodles of gore • Blood sucking competitions
• Dancing to the Grave Full Dead
• Hourly plasma-tasting sessions with the *Gory Times*
blood buff, Miroslav Slurp
• Wolf obedience demonstrations
• Comedy from vampire stand-up, Clumsy Clot
• Soya-based blood products (for vegetarian vampires)
• Demonstration of new Factor 10,000 sunblock
• Grim Estates display of nightmare castles for rent or sale
• The Ideal Coffin Exhibition

**Dress: Traditional; cloaks, big collars, pointy boots
etc. Strictly no jeans or trainers
Official language: English
All not to be missed (or else!)
Click the bats for arrangements re time and place.**

'Brilliant!' gasped Sandy. 'This has just got to be the huge something that Professor Weatherwax was on about. Now he can sort them once and for all! All we need now is the place and time. Quick, Jason – click a bat!'

Jason aimed his cursor arrow at one of the two bats that were fluttering madly around the edges of the advert. As he clicked, a large banner unfurled from behind the bat's body. On it was written . . .

'That's this Sunday!' exclaimed Sandy.

'The sixth of November is the date in *Dracula* when the Count gets killed by Jonathan Harker and his pals!' exclaimed Claire. 'This must be some sort of anniversary!'

'Brilliant!' said Poppy. 'Now all we need is the place. Then we'll have cracked it!'

Jason clicked on the other bat. A second later a message appeared which said . . .

47

> Arrangements:
> Venue: Englandland
> Exact location will be passed on by usual networks.
> Use codeword when making contact.

'Oh shucks!' said Jason. 'This means it could all be over and finished while we're still trying to discover its location!'

'What does "will be passed on by the usual networks" mean?' said Darren.

'It'll be like those huge rave parties that my big brother used to go,' said Sandy. 'The exact place isn't announced until the very last moment. Then it gets passed on in a cascade.'

'So do they all get together in an amusement hall?' said Darren.

'That's an arcade, Darren,' said Claire. 'A cascade's when one person tells two or three people and each of them tells three more, and so on until everyone knows. It's to cut down the chances of the police finding out and putting a stop to things.'

'Or in this case, Professor Weatherwax and his team,' said Poppy.

'This announcement will have been up on the website for some time now,' said Sandy. 'Which is obviously why they all came to

England in the first place. They must have been given the general area since – otherwise they wouldn't have come to the Eck Valley.'

'But if we know the area,' said Darren, 'why can't we just go there nobble them all?

'Because the Eck Valley's ginormous, Darren,' said Poppy. 'Our parents' farm covers a thousand acres! Moaning Man Moor is about eight thousand. It would be like looking for a needle in haystack. The only people who'll know the exact spot will be Bruno and Hildegard, and their inner circle of vampire helpers.'

'And their kids,' said Darren.

'I wonder if Vladimir would tell us?' said Rose.

'I doubt it,' said Claire. 'He might be a bit rebellious and want to be like a normal human teenager, but he's still a born vampire. Anyway, for all we know he might still be Dalmatian-shaped.' She looked thoughtful for a moment then said, 'I'll tell you someone who might have some idea where the event's going to be.'

'Who?' said the Vigilantes.

'My Grandpa Reg,' said Claire.

Chapter Five
The Grandpire

'But I thought he was half-vampirized,' said Sandy.

'That's all the more reason for him to know something,' said Claire. 'Don't forget, he showed the Blodvats their underground hidey holes in the first place. They probably felt perfectly free to talk in front of him, especially as he was already under their influence. If we chat to him, he might just let something slip. Even the tiniest clue might help.'

'You're right!' said Jason. 'It's definitely worth a try. How is he, anyway, Claire?'

'Actually, he's a lot worse,' said Claire. 'My dog, Wendy, still won't go anywhere near him. If they happen to bump into each other Wendy just backs off snarling. I think the Blodvats have been at him again.'

'But why?' said Rose. 'He's told them

where the hidey holes are. They've got his sausage-making machine, and his blood! What else could they want?'

'His secret prize-winning recipes!' said Claire. 'They definitely haven't finished with him. I'm sure they got to him on Hallowe'en night. He's been acting tons weirder since then. This morning he jumped out from behind a big shrub and got Cyril, our postman.'

'An ambush!' exclaimed Poppy.

'No, holly,' said Claire. 'Anyway, Cyril just twanged him with an elastic band and scurried off.'

'Do you think Hildegard's still – err, you know – guzzling him?' said Rose.

'Oh, definitely. His neck's got that many fang marks it's beginning to look like a second-hand dartboard,' said Claire. 'Mum and dad think it's because he shakes so much when he's shaving. But I know better. Although I suppose refusing to use a mirror doesn't help. He won't go near them!'

Poppy took out her *Undead: the Facts* vampire book then said, 'It says here that all true vampires hate mirrors. It's something to do with them not having reflections.'

'If you looked like the Blodvats you

wouldn't want a reflection,' said Sandy. 'That mirror business is worrying, isn't it, Claire?'

'Very. I know Professor Weatherwax said that Grandpa's only a shampire and he's resisting full vampirization, but I'm scared he'll soon become the real thing. Then there's no telling what will happen!'

'If it was the old days they'd cut off his head with a grave-digger's spade,' said Rose.

'Or drive enormous red-hot nails into his brain,' added Poppy. 'Look, here's how they did it!' She flicked to a terrifying print of some peasants hammering gigantic, glowing nails into the skull of a rather confused and unhappy-ooking vampire. Claire appeared to be on the verge of tears.

'Steady on!' said Sandy. 'This is Claire's grandpa, not some red-eyed, blood-crazed monster. Well, not yet, he isn't.'

'Sorry, Claire!' said Poppy. 'We didn't mean to upset you.'

Jason said, 'From what you've told us, Claire, I don't think there's any point in just chatting to Grandpa Reg in the hope he'll let something slip. I think we've got to take some drastic action. And I mean *drastic*. We're going to have to try and de-vampirize him.'

All the other Vigilantes gasped.

'Isn't that really dangerous?' said Sandy.

'It can be,' said Jason. 'But it sounds like he's almost past the point of no return. Claire, he's *your* grandpa. What do you think?'

Claire thought long and hard. 'I think you're right. As long as we don't try anything too risky. I just wish the Professor was around to help us.'

'So how do we do this de-vampirizing then?' said Sandy.

Poppy opened her book, and said, 'Look, it shows you here. The most effective way is probably to completely drain the victim of their own blood, then refill them with fresh, uncontaminated blood. But I think that might be just a bit too tricky for us lot. We'd probably best go for the down to earth approach.'

'What's that?' asked Sandy.

'The victim has to eat some soil from the resting place of the Undead.'

'Are you saying we take him to a vampire's grave then say, "Hmm yummy soil! Do you fancy a couple of mouthfuls, Grandpa Reg?"' said Jason. 'Look, Poppy, I know Claire's grandpa is seventy-five and semi-doolally but I really can't see him wanting to go down on his hands and knees and gobble up earth.'

Darren suddenly looked thoughtful. 'He wouldn't need to – we could mix some grave soil in a bowl of tomato soup so he doesn't know it's there. My mum says the tomato soup from Chumley Co-op tastes just like muck anyway.'

'Absolutely brilliant!' said Jason. 'I'm beginning to think that you're not just a pair of hideous lime green day-glo trainers after all!'

'They're avocado,' said Darren.

'There is one other thing,' said Poppy. 'For de-vampirizing to be fully effective, with no risks of the victim ever being turned back into a vampire, it must be soil from resting place of the vampire that did the biting.'

'It's got to be Hildegard,' said Claire. 'It'll be her grave soil we need!'

'So where's she been going to ground?' said Sandy.

'She kips in the back of the Blodmobile as far as we know,' said Jason. 'The only proper grave we've seen is Vladimir's. But he hasn't actually bitten Claire's grandpa. At least, we don't think he has.'

'How are we going to get soil from Hildegard's grave if all she's done is sleep in the Blodmobile?' said Rose.

Claire suddenly had an idea. 'Sandy, do you remember telling us you'd seen the Blodvats getting in their coffins and that as Bruno chucked soil on them both some fell on the grass? Did it actually go on Hildegard first?'

'I think so!' said Sandy. 'Come to think of it, she even bunged some of it out of her box, after he'd overfilled her.'

'I'm sure that would count as soil from the resting place of a vampire,' said Claire.

'It's worth a try,' said Jason. 'I don't suppose you happen to remember exactly where these little heaps of muck were?'

'Somewhere in Five Acre Woods,' said Sandy. 'Quite near to Eckton Lane.'

'Lead the way, Sandy,' said Poppy. 'Or should we call you Soily?'

Half an hour later all six Vigilantes were crawling around on their hands and knees in Five Acre Woods.

'All these bushes and trees look the same,' said Sandy, 'but I'm sure this is where the

Blodmobile was parked. I think these are the tyre tracks.' Then he suddenly said, 'Got it!' and pointed to some scattered earth on the grass.

'There's not much, is there?' said Rose.

'It's enough!' said Poppy. 'We're not planning to make him eat a wheelbarrow full!'

Sandy scooped some of the earth into an empty yoghurt pot then held it out for the others to see. 'Look!' he said. 'I know it's the right stuff because it's the colour of—'

'Coffee,' said Claire.

'Great,' said Jason. 'Now all we've got to do is get Grandpa Reg to eat the stuff!'

The Vigilantes gathered in the Whimsys' kitchen to watch Claire stir several spoonfuls of genuine Tonsilveinian earth into a steaming bowl of Chumley Co-op cream of tomato soup.

When the Vigilantes had made their way up the stairs, Claire tapped lightly on Grandpa Reg's door and said, 'Hi, Grandpa! It's me. I've brought you your soup. And I've got some pals with me. Is it all right if we come in?'

'Darkness!' groaned a voice from inside the bedroom. 'The black bat flaps, the vein tears, the gore gushes. Like nectar! Ah! *Zullabtervok! Ven letch ilvarter sprak!*'

'Sorry Grandpa?' said Claire. 'I didn't quite catch all of that?'

'*Martossnachter!*' replied the voice. Then, more urgently, '*Und villy villy snodtak!*'

The Vigilantes exchanged looks of terror and amazement. The voice didn't sound like Grandpa Reg. It was more coarse and grating, like someone pouring gravel into a saucepan – and possibly foreign.

But then another voice, immediately recognizable, said, 'Yer daft twerp! Get yerself down the Pudding Makers fer a skinful wi' the lads!'

'That's definitely Grandpa!' said Claire.

'He must have someone with him.'

'But who?' whispered Poppy.

Rose put her hand over her mouth and said, 'Could it be a vam—?'

'I dunno,' said Claire. 'But we ought to get in there quick. They may be about to do something horrid!'

'Bring me the brides of Nosferatu!' croaked the stranger. *'Portant muk zen higglen den Nosferatu!'*

Claire didn't waste another moment. 'Here goes!' she said. She pushed open the door and the Vigilantes entered the room. Grandpa Reg was standing by his bed. He had combed his few remaining wisps of hair straight up in the middle of his skull so that it resembled a very mean-looking, but rather low-key, Mohican. His face was daubed all over with Mrs Whimsy's cold cream and he had an old red sheet slung around his shoulders. Underneath it he was wearing his string vest and the black leotard that Claire's mum wore to her aerobics class, while his legs and feet were clad in her red leg warmers and his best fishing Wellingtons.

'Ah! Perishables vak snat urgellvurm!' he snarled, the moment he saw them. Then,

spotting the Mason twins, he added, *'Ah zen higglen den Nosferatu!'*

Two things immediately became apparent. One was that he hadn't recognized any of them, and the other was that there had been no one else in the room with him.

Suddenly he scratched himself under his armpit, yawned, then – in his familiar Grandpa Reg voice – said, 'Come to think of it, I couldn't half fancy a pint of Old Indigestible. P'raps I will pop down t' Pudding Makers?' But then his eyes began to glow an alarming shade of red and he growled, *'Ven futz Pudding Makers iz voss kok kok kok!'* and started slapping himself on the side of the head!

'He's gone!' gasped Jason.

'Flipped!' said Sandy.

'It's that struggle the Professor was on about!' gasped Claire. 'Grandpa's good inner self is battling with his evil vampire one!'

'Which one's winning?' whispered Sandy.

'I'd put my money on the vampire,' said Jason.

'Perhaps we're too late,' said Rose. 'Maybe he's already a vampire?'

'Or even a Grandpire?' said Darren.

Suddenly Grandpa Reg began to advance, his eyes glowing even redder. The Vigilantes backed away. However, Rose became isolated from the others and found herself cornered.

Grandpa Reg's eyes fixed on her and he slowly crept forwards, a look of total evil spreading across his extremely creamy face.

'Ah!' he sighed. *'Und higglen den Nosferatu!'*

'No, I'm not!' cried Rose. 'I'm Rose Mason from Sunny Brook Farm.'

As she began to whimper pitifully, Grandpa Reg snarled and curled back his top lip. Although this wasn't quite as frightening as it would have been if he'd had his false teeth in, the sight of his naked pink gums and the trail of drool that trickled down his chin still made it very disturbing. When he was within striking distance he suddenly lunged at Rose, slobbering and snarling, but at that same moment there was a sharp *Twanggg!* noise, then something small and brown flew through the air and struck him behind the ear with a satisfying *Thwokk!* sound.

Grandpa Reg staggered backwards, sat down on his bed, then put his hand on his ear and yelled 'By the cringe! What the flippin' 'eck were that?'

'One of these,' said Darren, holding up a couple of elastic bands. 'I spotted them on your front drive.'

'Nice one, Darren!' said Poppy.

Claire looked at her grandpa. He was still shocked, so she quickly stepped forward with the bowl of soup 'n' soil.

'Grandpa, I've got your soup here,' she said.

Grandpa Reg stared at her in bewilderment, until a vague glimmer of recognition came into his eyes. He said, 'Oh right, lass . . . err, ta very much!' Then he took the soup straight from her and began to spoon it down like he'd not eaten for a week. Two seconds later the bowl and spoon slipped from his hands and crashed to the bedroom floor. Grandpa Reg flopped back on to the bed, apparently dead to the world.

'Oh no!' screamed Claire. 'We've only gone and killed him!'

He certainly looked dead. Under the thick layer of cold cream his skin had turned a delicate shade of blue, his eyes and mouth were wide open and he didn't appear to be showing any signs of life whatsoever.

'You and your bright ideas, Jason!' cried Poppy. 'Now look what you've gone and done!'

'I'm sorry, Claire,' gasped Jason. 'I wouldn't have suggested trying to de-vampirize him if I'd thought anything like this would happen!'

A second later Grandpa Reg sat up, looked at his watch and said, 'Blimey! Is that the time! I'm only missin' the bloomin' cricket on telly!'

As the Vigilantes all breathed yet another sigh of relief Claire made a huge effort to pull herself together. She said, 'Actually, I think the cricket's finished for the season, Grandpa.'

'What month is it?' said Grandpa Reg.

'November,' said Claire.

'You what—' said Grandpa Reg. 'So where's blinkin' September gone then? And October?' Then he happened to notice his black leotard and Wellington ensemble and, almost passing out a second time, said, 'What the—?'

Half an hour later Grandpa Reg was back in his normal clothes and, with a little help from the other Vigilantes, Claire told him the whole story of his time as a shampire and his near conversion to complete vampirism.

'Well, I'll be jiggered!' he said. 'Do you know, I can't remember a blinking thing about any of it! The past few weeks are just a huge blank in my mind!'

'Nothing?' said Claire. 'Not even reading your Westerns and staying in bed?'

Grandpa thought hard for a moment then said, 'Now you come to mention it, I do. But it's blurry and mixed up, like some weird dream!'

'What about the time you felt better and went to the Pudding Maker's Arms?' said Claire.

Grandpa Reg scratched his head and narrowed his eyes. Suddenly he looked terribly guilty and said, 'It's coming back to me now. I can remember something to do with plastic teeth. And being inside a big wheely bin. Oo-er, Claire! I think I might have done something bad!'

'No, you haven't, Grandpa,' said Claire. 'It's *them* who are bad!'

'It was the voices!' said Grandpa Reg. 'Hildegard's and Bruno's. They were in my head. Telling me to pretend to be better. So that I could go out and bite people. But I didn't really want to!'

'Don't worry, Grandpa Reg!' said Claire. 'That's all over now. We need you to think about that time you went out in the Blodvats' big car. Try to remember if you heard or saw anything unusual.'

'It's really important,' said Sandy. 'People's lives depend on it!'

'All right!' said Grandpa Reg. 'I'll do me best.' He pressed his fist to his forehead then scrunched up his face in concentration. After a minute he suddenly sat up straight, snapped his fingers, and said, 'Yes! Yes! It's all coming back to me now!'

Claire grasped his hand and said, 'And did you see or hear anything unusual?'

Grandpa Reg thought hard for a moment, then said, 'No – not a thing.'

'Oh dear,' said Claire. 'Are you sure?'

'I'm certain of it!' said Grandpa Reg.

The Vigilantes shook their heads in despair.

'But I did the next time,' he said.

Claire and the Vigilantes jumped, as though they'd just been stung by giant bees.

'*What?*' Claire cried. 'What next time? You only went out with them once!'

'No, I didn't,' said Grandpa Reg. 'We went out loads of times. It was our secret. Bruno and Hildegard came and picked me up when you were at school and Mum and Dad were at the factory. We went all over the place! Ravenscrag, the Catacombs, Crawley Common, Moaning Man Cavern. And wherever we went the other ones would be there too.'

'What other ones?' said Claire. 'Do you mean vampires?'

Grandpa Reg scratched his head then said, 'I suppose they would be! Their teeth were certainly big enough. They were like worker vampires, forever digging and shifting boxes of soil. And there were these three lasses and a hideous big lad! Always jigging, he was! And then there was the other little one.'

'What other little one?' said Claire. 'Do you mean Hildegard?'

''Course not!' said Grandpa. 'It was a little bloke! Not a vampire, though. I think they called him Wolf-something-or-other. I saw him the second time they took me to Ravenscrag. He was scrabbling around on his hands and knees, like he was looking for something.'

'The dust!' gasped Sandy.

'Yes, that was it!' said Grandpa Reg. 'They kept saying it was the dust of the Master and they just had to have it. They even asked me if I knew where it was. I hadn't a clue what they were talking about. They kept saying, "Have you found it?" And Wolfgang would shake his head, looking absolutely terrified, and the whippet would say, "He lies!"

'Once they got so angry that Bruno lifted him off the ground and shook him that hard I thought his brains would fall out! I didn't half feel sorry for him! Poor little Wolfgang.'

'Was that definitely what they called him?' said Claire.

'Yes,' said Grandpa Reg, 'but I know for a fact that wasn't his real name.'

'Why?' said Claire excitedly.

'I just knew I knew him from somewhere!'

'Who was it?' gasped Claire. 'Who was it?'

Grandpa Reg slowly rubbed his chin. 'To tell you the

truth it's gone straight out of my mind! It's a complete blank.'

'But you've got to remember, Grandpa Reg,' cried Jason. 'It's important!'

'No, Jason!' said Claire. 'We can't force him. He'll never remember that way!' Then she looked at her Grandpa. 'Don't worry. Try thinking about something else, like all those places you visited. Was there one that seemed particularly important to Bruno and Hildegard?'

Grandpa Reg thought for a moment then said, 'Yes there was. I remember the first time we went there, I said, "You can't go 'ere!" and Hildegard said, "Oh yes ve can."'

'But why did you tell them they couldn't go there?' said Claire.

'Because of the whopping great fence and the Keep Out signs!' said Grandpa Reg. 'Yes, it was that old army place up in Eck Forest, where the soldiers used to do their training. And before that it was where they kept the German prisoners when the war was on. I tried to tell them it belonged to the government but Bruno just laughed and said, "That is why we are here, Mr Sausage. Sir Norman has given it to us!" Then he unlocked the big gates and we drove straight in. There were vampires, building this huge stage and repairing the shed where they used to keep the war prisoners.'

'I know that place!' cried Sandy. 'It would be perfect! The trees go nearly all the way round it, and it's really well-hidden at the bottom of that huge hollow they call the Devil's Wash Basin. It would be really hard to spot, even from the air!'

'I think you're probably right,' said Claire. She turned to her granddad and said, 'Thanks, Grandpa Reg. You've been absolutely brilliant.'

'Does that mean I can stop now?' said Grandpa Reg. 'I'm worn out.'

'Of course you can,' said Claire. 'We've got to go now. We've urgent business to attend to!'

Even as the Vigilantes were piling out of his bedroom, Grandpa Reg's eyes were beginning to close. But just as Claire turned to shut the door, he suddenly opened them and said, 'Oh yes – there's something else!'

'What!' said Claire. 'Have you remembered something about this Wolfgang?'

'No,' said Grandpa Reg. 'I was just wondering if you'd happened to video any of the cricket?'

Chapter Six

The Blood Shed

rabbing their bikes the Vigilantes set off for Eck Forest and after forty minutes' hard pedalling they reached the track that led into the woods. Soon they came to the big signs that stood by the entrance gates to the old army training camp.

'Are you sure this is a good idea?' said Jason as they hid their bikes and made their way over to the big perimeter fence. 'I mean, couldn't we have just e-mailed the Professor and told him to send his men up here?'

'No,' said Claire. 'At this stage we don't want to be sending the Professor on wild goose chases. We'll check it out for ourselves. Then we'll let him know.'

The entrance gates were padlocked but it didn't take long to find a section of the fence where wild animals had dug their way under it.

'OK!' said Claire. 'I'm going down to take a look around.'

'I'll come with you!' said Poppy.

'Fine,' said Claire. 'You lot hang around here and keep a lookout.' And with that the two girls wriggled under the fence and began to make their way towards the steep, wooded hillside that surrounded the Devil's Wash Basin. They hadn't gone far when they began to hear noises coming from the valley below.

'OK, Poppy!' muttered Claire. 'Follow me down and try not to make a sound.'

Poppy nodded and they started slithering and scrambling their way through the tangle of bushes and dead bracken. After a couple of hundred metres, the going became slightly easier. They paused to catch their breath and get the lie of the land. Just below was the roof of a huge wooden shed and, beyond that, an enormous open area, which was bordered by more sheds and what looked like a large concrete bunker. Claire pointed to the nearest and biggest shed and Poppy nodded.

Then they began the last part of their descent, finally clambering down a steep bank which ended at the rear wall of the big shed. Set in the wall, just a few metres away, was an open window. They reached it, stood on tiptoes and peered in. Then they gasped in horror!

Directly opposite, almost half the length of the wall, was an enormous cage. It was packed with dozens and dozens of wretched-looking men and women. Their faces were deathly white; their clothes filthy, with collars and sleeves torn where the vampires had hurriedly attempted to get at a vein. One man was attached to a huge drip and watched helplessly as his own blood trickled very, very slowly into a large glass flask. Two more were linked to an ancient suction pump that rattled and gurgled as it slowly squirted their blood into a small wooden barrel.

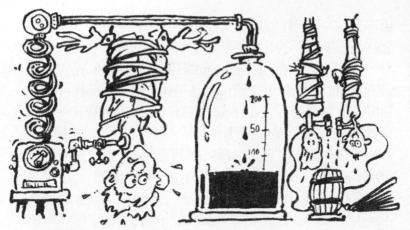

Moving amongst them were thuggish-looking, shaven-headed vampire guards, armed with long spiked sticks. Each gruesome ghoul was covered in horrendous tattoos while all manner of rings, studs and safety pins dangled and protruded from their hideously pierced ears, noses and lips. Occasionally, one of them would cruelly prod a captive and laugh heartlessly as the victim cried out in pain.

'Those poor people!' whispered Poppy. 'This is terrible. We've just got to help them!'

There was a sudden flurry of activity and two figures appeared in the doorway at the far end of the shed. They were Bruno and Hildegard Blodvat. They made their way towards the cage. The vampire guards immediately stood to attention and made that strange salute that Claire had first seen at Ravenscrag.

'Velcome to the Blood Shed, Ubervampires Blodvat!' said the biggest and most ferocious-looking of the guards. 'Or should I say, ze milking parlour, ha ha ha!'

'Oh, Otto!' screeched Hildegard. 'You are such a vag! You are tickling me pink!'

'Ha ha ha!' chuckled Bruno. 'Yes, very good, Otto! Ha ha! I am so much liking your jokings. Now, how is the blooding going?'

Otto gestured towards a huge collection of blood-filled bottles that stood against the end wall. He said, 'See, Ubervampire Bruno. We now have many litres! Soon there will be enough for the sausage-making!'

'Good! Good!' said Bruno. He peered into the giant cage, smiled cruelly and said, 'Now, let us be picking a Perishable that is good and ripe.' His evil eyes travelled from one terrified captive to another until they rested on a large, roly-poly man slumped at the back of the cage. He was staring at his feet quite miserably, as if he truly believed his end was near. Bruno pointed to him and said, 'THAT ONE!'

'Yesssss!' hissed Hildegard. 'A good choice, my Brunyplops! Very succulent!' As she said the word "succulent", bubbles of saliva frothed from the corners of her mouth. Bruno clicked his fingers and two of the shaven-headed vampires began pushing their way through the petrified captives. When they reached the man, he seemed to snap out of his trance, then he looked up at them in pure terror.

'It's Dr Grainger!' whispered Claire.

The thugs seized Dr Grainger by his ears and dragged him out of the cage. They hauled him to his feet, and with one swift, merciless movement, ripped off his shirt and trousers as if they were made of tissue paper. Trembling, his spare rolls of flesh wobbling pathetically, Dr Grainger stood before the Blodvats dressed only in his pants and socks. Hildegard reached for his arm and with the same black, talon-like fingernails that had stroked Claire's neck so creepily all those weeks before, she pinched his ample flesh, causing him to cry out in pain!

'Hmm – yesss!' she snarled. 'Very juiceeey!' She gave a short clap and a vampire appeared, carrying a bucket.

'What are they going to do to him?' gasped Poppy.

'I don't know,' muttered Claire. 'But it

won't be pleasant!'

Hildegard took something long and brown and slimy from the bucket. Something that wriggled and twitched and thrashed. With a look of pure pleasure on her evil little face she pressed it against Dr Grainger's arm. When she withdrew her hand the brown slimy thing was still firmly attached to his flesh.

'UURGH!' gasped Poppy. 'That's disgusting! It's a leech!'

Compared with what was about to happen, it was nothing. As the girls were almost sick with horror, Hildegard reached into the bucket, took out another leech, then pressed it against Dr Grainger's throat. His eyes stared wildly down at the horrible creatures

that clung remorselessly to his skin and greedily sucked out his life blood. There was nothing he could do, because the two thugs were holding him firmly by his wrists. As Bruno and Hildegard pressed yet more leeches on to his trembling flesh there was a squeal of excitement and their three despicable daughters came skipping into the shed.

'Hmmm!' cried Diptheria. 'That looks fun! What are you doing to him, Mommyblod?'

'We are trying out a clever idea of your daddy's,' crooned Hildegard, as she stuck another leech on Dr Grainger's huge stomach. 'For making the novelty nibblings to be enjoyed at our great event.'

'What do you do with them?' squeaked Scrofula.

'I will show you!' laughed Bruno. Then, pointing to the first leech that Hildegard had attached to Dr Grainger's flesh, he said, 'This one is nearly ready!' He started to peel the leech off Dr Grainger's arm, just as if he was removing a very large and awkward sticking plaster. After a short struggle and some very disturbing screaming from the doctor, the monstrous leech gave up its grip and came away in Bruno's hand with a horrible *ssssskrrrrp!* Bruno held it up for all to see. It was now at least twice its original size and had turned to a deep, rich red.

'Hmm,' said Bruno. 'The gorgeous gore juice. I think I am feeling a little bit thirsty!' He held the bloated creature above his head,

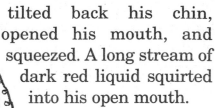

tilted back his chin, opened his mouth, and squeezed. A long stream of dark red liquid squirted into his open mouth.

'Uuurgh!' groaned Claire. 'I think I'm going to puke!'

'Oooh! Ooh!' cried Diptheria. 'What fun! Can I have some please, Daddyblod?'

And then her two sisters began jumping up and down and squealing, 'Yes! Yes! Me too! Me too!'

'Wait!' said Bruno. 'It is not just for drinkings!' He tossed the leech high into the air, and neatly caught it between his teeth. He chewed it ferociously, before swallowing the lot in one huge gulp. Then, as he let out a long and satisfied 'Buuuurp!', Hildegard and the girls immediately burst into wild applause.

'Hmmm, what fun!' cried Hildegard. 'I think that maybe we will be selling this for five Dracmares a squvirting!'

As Bruno's eyes crossed and uncrossed,

he burped, and said, 'Oh dear, I am veeling fery squiffy!' The squirt of AB-negative was obviously taking effect. 'OK!' he giggled, turning to the guards. 'Put him back but first take off the sucking-vurms and give them to my lovely girlsh. And be having shome for yourshelfs. Shey are on me!'

'No, they are on *him*!' laughed awful Otto. 'Ha ha ha!' Then he ripped a leech off Dr Grainger and tossed it to Diptheria, who began sucking it as though it were a very juicy orange.

When Dr Grainger was back in the cage Claire turned to Poppy, ashen-faced and shaken. 'I think we've seen enough! Come on. While they're all having fun we'll have a quick snoop around, then get back to the others.'

The two girls ducked down and made their way along the rear of the shed. As they turned the corner at the far end they found themselves a few metres away from an enormous wooden stage. Kneeling at its base was a small figure with its back to them. It was slowly hammering nails into one of the massive structure's supporting wooden beams. It only took Claire a moment to recognize the hammerer. It was Mr Pither!

She quickly scanned the huge open area in front of the platform and saw that there was no one else around. After signalling Poppy to follow she crept over to Mr Pither and tapped him lightly on the shoulder.

Mr Pither whirled around. 'Claire!' he gasped. 'What on earth are you doing here?'

'It's a long story,' said Claire. 'Too long to tell now. Let's move away so we can talk.'

Once they were hidden behind a large pile of timber, Claire said, 'Mr Pither, I'm so so glad to see you! Are you all right?'

Mr Pither sighed. 'Well, considering the circumstances, I'm not bad at all.' He nodded towards the Blood Shed. 'I'm certainly in better shape than those poor wretches. They've got your grandpa's pudding machine in there.' He pointed to the bunker. 'They call it the Pudding Bunker. That's where they're going to make the blood sausages.'

Claire glanced at Mr Pither's neck then said, 'But haven't they, err—'

'Bitten me?' said Mr Pither. 'No! Apparently my blood's not to their taste.'

'Then you must be blood group B-negative!' said Poppy.

'I am,' said Mr Pither. 'How did you know?'

'We've learned a lot about the undead and their nasty habits,' said Claire.

'Me, too!' said Mr Pither. 'The Blodvats have been holding me captive for weeks.'

'But why did they take you?' said Claire.

'It was all because of a story I wrote,' said Mr Pither. 'Something I did for fun. It was a sort of follow-up to *Dracula*. I published it on a little website. I even gave myself a silly name. I called myself Wolfgang Winklemann.'

'So *you're* Wolfgang!' exclaimed Claire.

'It's my pen name,' explained Mr Pither. 'The story was just something I made up on the spur of the moment. Saying how Jonathan Harker and his pals had put Dracula's remains in a box and had battled their way back across Europe then hidden it in a secret location, somewhere between Chumley and Whitby. The Blodvats came across it when they were surfing the net. And they believed every word of it! That's why they came to our school and talked to me. They said that I had to tell them where the box of dust was. I kept trying to explain that it was just fiction, but they wouldn't believe me! They didn't even seem to actually know what fiction was!'

'I heard you talking to Bruno, but I thought

you were saying "friction"!' said Claire.

'They'd got it into their heads that this box was hidden somewhere up at Ravenscrag,' continued Mr Pither. 'The night after they'd been into school, they came for me and took me up there. I've been totally in their power ever since! That crazy story has certainly landed me in lots of trouble!'

'But haven't you tried to escape?' said Poppy.

'No,' said Mr Pither. 'They said that if I did they'd do something really bad to a child from Chumley Primary. And I knew they meant it. They've had me running around helping them make preparations for this huge gathering they're planning. That's what I was doing when you saw me at Ravenscrag. I had to organize the arrival of that sailing ship and the coach and horses. But the main thing they've had me doing is looking for the box. I've given up trying to tell them it doesn't exist. Now I just pretend to look for it! But I know I've only got a couple of days left.'

'Listen, Mr Pither,' said Claire. 'It's really important that you find that box. For the sake of those people and for the kids of Chumley. We've made contact with people who are in a position to make big problems for the Blodvats! But they and their hordes have all got to be in the one place at the same time. Finding the box would more or less guarantee that they will be.'

'But how can I find it,' said Mr Pither, 'if it doesn't exist? I can't magic it out of thin air!'

'*We* can!' said Claire. 'We can make sure you do find it. Just tell us when and where you're going to be searching.'

'They're taking me up to Ravenscrag again tomorrow afternoon,' said Mr Pither. 'They say it's my last chance. And after that they say they'll drain a Perishable dry. Perhaps a child!'

'OK,' said Claire. 'We'll make sure it's there. Do you remember where Jason and I bumped into you that day?'

'Yes, it was by that big tombstone with the eagle carved on it.'

'We'll bury it just beneath the turf next to that,' said Claire. 'On the side nearest the sea.'

'Yes, OK!' said Mr Pither. 'But what about the captives in the Blood Shed?'

'Don't worry about them,' said Claire. 'Or yourself. The people we're working with are experts in dealing with the Undead. Now that we know where the event's going to take place

83

it'll simply be a matter of them coming up here and zapping the vamps. Then you and all those people will finally be free!'

When the girls reached the hole under the fence the other Vigilantes looked relieved to see them. Claire quickly told them how it was really important for them to get the box of dust up to Ravenscrag.

'But I thought we were doing that with the Professor?' said Jason.

'We were,' said Claire. 'But it's fifty times more urgent now. We'll have to sort it ourselves!'

'We'll need a box and some dust, then,' said Sandy.

'We've got a really old biscuit tin at home,' said Poppy. 'It was our great-great-gran's. Mum only uses it on special occasions so I'm sure she wouldn't miss it! We could fill it with dust from the bag on our vacuum cleaner.'

'Perfect!' said Claire. 'OK, I'll leave that to you and Rose to sort first thing tomorrow. Jason will show you where to bury it. Take Darren and Sandy with you – they can act as lookouts. Then, if you can, get yourselves hidden and watch to make sure they find it. Come to my place once you've got it all sorted. My mum and dad will be out shopping so we can plan our next moves.'

'What will you be doing while we're up at Ravenscrag?' said Sandy.

'I'll be e-mailing Professor Weatherwax and letting him know everything we've found out today,' said Claire. 'All the things he'll need to know in order to organize a successful attack and rescue operation. We mustn't leave anything to chance. We mustn't fail.'

Chapter
Seven

Nandor Does His Stuff

The following afternoon Claire was sitting in her bedroom, frantically clicking the Internet e-mail icon on her computer desktop when she heard the front door bell ring. Grandpa Reg was out in the garden with Wendy, so she leapt up and raced down to open the door. The Vigilantes were standing on her front step, looking extremely pleased with themselves.

'How did it go?' said Claire, as she let them into the hall.

'Absolutely brilliant!' said Sandy.

'We buried the tin full of vacuum cleaner dust, then stayed around to see what happened,' said Rose.

'Yep!' said Jason. 'After about three quarters of an hour the Blodvats turned up with Mr Pither. He handed them the biscuit tin, and cor – you should have seen their faces! Bruno was so pleased that he gave Mr Pither a big smacking kiss on top of his head then picked him up and swung him around like a three-year-old!'

'So that's that, then!' said Sandy. 'All that's got to happen now is for the Professor and his people to get their team up to the Devil's Wash Basin, then catch the Blodvats and their bloodsucker buddies mid-celebration and zap the whole pongy lot of them. Brilliant!'

'Actually,' said Claire, 'I don't think it's going to be that simple.'

'Why?' said Poppy. 'Is there a problem?'

'A big one,' said Claire. 'It's the Professor. He's not answered any of my e-mails. It's as if he's vanished from the face of the earth.'

'What about his telephone?' said Jason.

'I keep getting "Number Unobtainable".'

'We could go to the police and tell them,' said Darren.

'We definitely can't. Not yet,' said Claire. 'It would take yonks to convince them. And if they *did* believe us, they'd probably go charging up there, batons drawn and sirens screaming. The vamps would spot them a mile off, transform themselves, and be off like a shot!'

'You're right,' said Poppy. 'And if they did leave in a panic, there's no telling what they'd do to those people and Mr Pither before they went. Probably something *really* terrible.'

'And it would all be our fault,' said Claire. 'Anyway, there's still a chance the Professor will turn up. We can't let him down. We're Vampire Vigilantes!'

'So what are we going to do?' said Sandy.

'I've got a plan!' said Claire. 'It's simple, but tricky: we sabotage the blood puddings. Remember I told you that Bruno threw that huge wobbly when he bit into Grandpa Reg's triple garlic special? The one thing vampires hate more than anything is garlic. So all we've got to do is make sure a load of it goes into the blood pudding mixture before its final boiling. Once all the vamps have gobbled the garlicky goodies, they'll be at our mercy!'

'But what do we do *then*?' said Sandy. 'They're not going to stay nobbled by the garlic for ever.'

'A least that would give us a chance to save the people they're holding prisoner. And if Professor Weatherwax still hasn't turned up, that's when we call the cops. Once we show them the missing people and the banjaxed vamps they're hardly likely to accuse us of making the whole thing up.'

'Brilliant, Claire!' said Jason. 'So, all we've got to do now is decide who's going to sneak up there with the garlic and dump it in the blood pudding mix.'

'I'll do it!' said a voice behind them.

'Grandpa Reg!' said Claire. 'How long have you been standing there?'

'About three minutes,' said Grandpa Reg, as he stepped into the hall. 'I've more or less heard everything you've said. And it sounds to me like I'm the man for the job!'

'But you can't do it, Grandpa Reg,' protested Claire. 'You're old and frail!'

'I'm as tough as old boots,' said Grandpa Reg. 'That de-vamping has worked wonders. But Blubber Brain and Ferret Features don't know I'm de-vampirized. When they last saw me I was on the edge of becoming a fully-fledged bloodsucker. So I'll pretend I've gone all the way. And don't forget, ever since Licorice Legs and Gorilla Gob turned up they've been pestering me to tell them my secret recipes and rustle up the perfect human blood pudding for them. So that's what I'll do.' He winked and added,

'But with a few extra ingredients!'

'It's a good idea, Claire,' said Poppy. 'And now that Grandpa Reg has been de-vamped he'll be immune to their bites as well.'

Claire thought for a moment, then said, 'All right, Grandpa Reg. It's an excellent plan, I agree. But only as long as you're really, really careful. And there's one other condition.'

'I might have known it!' said Grandpa Reg. 'All right, what is it?'

'That I go with you!' said Claire. 'You're going need someone to watch your back. I've still got my vamp outfit from last year's Fright Night so I shouldn't have any problem sneaking into the vamp-camp. I'll blend in nicely.'

'What are we going to be doing while you're having fun up at the Devil's Wash Basin?' said Sandy.

'A couple of you stay here in Chumley,' said Claire. 'Jason, I think one of them should be you. Just keep checking your e-mails and trying the Professor's number. Darren can keep you company.'

'Aw! Do I have to?' said Darren. 'I was looking forward to some action.'

'I hadn't finished!' said Claire. 'If the Professor's still not made contact by five tomorrow afternoon, both of you go straight to the police and tell them everything. Then you get them to come to the Devil's Wash Basin. Even if it means stamping on their toes and making them chase you up there!'

'What about us?' said Poppy. 'What should we do?'

'Well,' said Claire. 'If all goes according to plan we'll need help getting those kidnapped people out of there. If you and Rose and Sandy are lurking nearby you can move in the moment we need you.'

'I've got an idea!' said Rose. 'Me and Poppy can go up there on our ponies!'

'If the people need extra help we could belt back down to our farm and get Dad to come up with a trailer or a lorry!' said Poppy.

'OK!' said Grandpa Reg. 'Does everyone know what they're doing?'

All the Vigilantes nodded.

'Right!' said Grandpa Reg. 'Here's to tomorrow!'

Grandpa Reg's arrival at the vamp camp the following afternoon was a triumph, both for him and for the the Blodvats. They were so overjoyed that they even gave him his own snazzy vampire costume, and a new name: from now he was to be known to his vampire brothers and sisters as Nandor the Bat! He and Hildegard and Bruno put on long white pudding makers' coats and made their way to Pudding Bunker in preparation for the pouring and stirring of the mixture.

Claire's entrance into the vampire stronghold wasn't quite so easy. Nevertheless, through a combination of courage and some very devious dodging and ducking, she manoeuvred her way to the Pudding Bunker where she joined the little crowd of vampires who were watching the gory action.

Grandpa Reg was hard at work directing odious Otto and his team of thugs as they loaded the stolen Plasmatic with the hundreds and hundreds of little sausage skins. Once all the skins were in place and a dozen extra big ones had been added for the Blodvats and their vampire favourites, Grandpa Reg (alias Nandor) raised his hands and said, 'Now for the blood!'

Otto and his team enthusiastically began sloshing the gore into the huge bloodbath that

was attached to one end of the Plasmatic. When every last drop of the liquid had been poured in and the bloodbath was three-quarters full, Grandpa Reg pointed to the bulging sacks of stolen pudding ingredients, and cried, 'Now for the stirring! Put in the oatmeal! And the barley! And all the rest!'

He handed two big wooden spoons to Bruno and Hildegard. As Otto and the thugs tipped in the ingredients, Hildegard and Bruno stuck in their megaspoons and began stirring furiously. A thick gooey mixture began to form and hiss . . .

After several minutes of non-stop

stirring, Hildegard cried, 'But Nandor! What about the secret ingredients? Isn't it time to be puttings them in?'

'Yes! Yes!' yelled Grandpa Reg. 'You are right! The time is perfect!' He stuck his finger deep into his left ear, waggled it about a bit, and brought out a huge and disgusting lump of bright yellow earwax which he calmly flicked into the bloodbath.

'Nandor!' exclaimed Bruno, as he watched the earwax slowly melt into the mixture. 'Is this being a secret special ingredient?'

'Oh yes!' said Grandpa Reg. 'It is for the flavour!'

This answer seemed to satisfy both Blodvats. Next Grandpa Reg leaned over the bubbling gloop and vigorously brushed his hair over it for a couple of minutes, causing a blizzard of dandruff to float down into the mixture. Then he glanced at the Blodvats and said, 'Also for the flavour!' They both looked at him with undisguised awe and admiration.

After that he reached into his pocket and scooped out its entire contents, including some torn bits of paper tissue, two paracetamol tablets, four dead bluebottles (left over from his fly-catching phase), an out-of-date bus pass, a breath freshener, and a lump of sticky toffee, then threw the whole lot in, taking the trouble to tell Bruno and Hildegard that these ingredients were 'For the texture,' which seemed to impress them no end.

Next he took out the bottle containing the cocktail of household liquids and powders he'd prepared the previous evening, which included super glue, ant killer, creosote, bath scourer, thick bleach and washing-up liquid. After telling the Blodvats it was 'For the colour!' he dolloped the whole lot in, and even got a round of applause for his efforts.

Finally he reached underneath his cape, seized the enormous bag of dried spices, chilli and triple-strength garlic that he and the Vigilantes had bought at Safeburies the previous afternoon, and emptied the whole lot in, yelling, 'For the nice surprise!' and, 'Stir faster!' as the last thing he wanted was for the vamps to get a good look at these last extra special additives.

As the whole caboodle disappeared under the foaming surface he raised his hands above his head and cried, 'It is done! It is done!' and the Blodvats threw their wooden spoons in the air and gave an enormous cheer.

Phew! thought Claire. At last! It's in!

'Now!' said Grandpa. 'We will begin the making!'

He pressed the big red button on the Plasmatic and the great machine suddenly began to whirr and shudder into life. There was a gurgling, slurping noise and the bloody goo began disappearing down the long tube that led to rows of shining nozzles. Soon the Plasmatic was humming and beeping and flashing and throbbing as the high speed

process finally got under way. Three minutes later dozens and dozens of ready cooled mini-Blodfurters began tumbling from the end of the Plasmatic into the giant baskets that Otto and his helpers held in readiness.

Grandpa Reg glanced at Claire and winked. Then he tapped his nose a couple of times. This was the signal she'd been waiting for. It was now time to begin phase two of their mission. So, with one last glance at the sausage harvesters she wandered out of the Pudding Bunker.

As Claire stepped out on to the massive parade ground about ten things hit her at once. The three most noticeable ones were the smell, the noise and the sheer amount of stinky vampire bodies that were packed into that huge space! The horrific din was made up of the yowling, chattering and screeching of the vampires. The crush was incredible. She could hardly move more than a few paces without getting a bony vampire elbow in her ribs or a vampire shoulder in her back.

Claire suddenly noticed a very large vampire clutching a bright silver micro-scooter. It was Vladimir! Just as she was thinking he might be about to put on a fantastic scootering display, two very large and boisterous vampires pushed their way in front of her and she lost sight of him.

Otto's thugs were now making their way through the crowd, passing out the first free sample of the Blodfurters to the excited revellers. As they handed over each sausage they would solemnly say, 'It is for the moment of the Master's return. Do not be biting until the signal!' The grateful vampires would nod obediently, then eagerly clutch their sausages to their chests.

Claire decided it was time to make her way to the shed where the captives were held. She needed to be there before all the vampires took their first bite of the spiked Blodfurters. However, try as she might, she was unable to resist the throng of surging bodies. After a couple of minutes she was at least fifty metres from where she wanted to be. She was hemmed in on all sides. All she could do now was go with the flow and hope for the best.

Gradually, the swaying and pushing subsided. The huge crowd could go no further. Nine hundred wildly excited vampires were tightly packed into the area in front of the stage. With Claire wedged firmly in the middle of them.

Claire looked up at the gigantic platform Perched at one end of the stage were twelve vampire musicians. They were creating the sort of noise that makes the most irritating car alarm sound soothing and melodious. Three were crouched at the front, screaming and yowling for all they were worth. Two more held a couple of vampire cats by their tails, tugging and twisting, causing the strange animals to caterwaul incessantly. Three others were repeatedly offering large bags of red sweets to some vampire children, only to snatch them away at the last second, thereby making the little vamp-brats bawl at the top of their voices.

All this was accompanied by a giant vampire clobbering a piece of rusty corrugated iron with a sledge-hammer, and a very mad looking vampire tearing the strings from an open grand piano with its bare teeth.

In front of the band was a large sign saying . . .

```
THE GRAVE FULL DEAD
UNDERGROUND MUSIC FROM OUT THERE
Requests Welcome
```

Despite being packed like sardines, hundreds of vampires were yowling ecstatically to the music, whilst spinning like dysfunctional CD-players and leaping up and down as if their feet had built-in super springs.

'They love it,' whispered a voice next to Claire. 'It's music to their ears.'

Chapter Eight
The Proof
of the
Pudding

laire turned to see who'd spoken. 'Cripes!' she said. 'Professor Weatherwax! Where did you come from?'

The Professor, who, like Claire, was dressed in a vampire outfit, raised his finger to his lips, then whispered, 'Little problem with Sir Norman and his pals. But it's sorted now. And so are they! I'll explain later. The main thing is I've made contact with your fellow Vigilantes. And my people are all in position.' Then he smiled, and said, 'But from what your friends have told me you don't seem to have been doing too badly without us. And thanks for the e-mail. Very useful!'

As half a dozen spinning, leaping, yowling vampires bounced past them he raised a tiny mobile phone to his mouth and said, 'Contact made with Vigilante one. Five minutes to resurrection. All units stand by!'

Slipping the phone into his inside pocket, he pointed to the stage and said, 'It looks like the main event is about to begin. Maybe we should prepare for fireworks.'

The stage was set for the return of the Master. In the centre was an enormous altar draped in black velvet behind which stood a large microphone on a stand. Just to one side of the stage, and standing in readiness for the return of the greatest vampire the world had ever known, was the sinister black coach and horses that Claire and Jason had first seen up at Ravenscrag. Next to them was a posh-looking coffin with a banner draped across it that said 'Welcome Back Drac' in many languages.

The Grave Full Dead suddenly fell silent. Then, as the giant vampire drummer slowly began to wallop his piece of corrugated tin and the lead yowlers blew a wet but extremely rousing fanfare of raspberries, Bruno and Hildegard made their entrance and began to climb the wooden steps that led to stage.

They had changed from the long white coats into black lurex jumpsuits with long black leather vampire capes. Hildy had topped off her outfit with a big fang-shaped hat that was decorated with at least five stuffed bats, making it look like she'd recently covered it in superglue, then walked through a particularly busy bat roost. Bruno was still wearing his horrendous hat with the feather in it, which didn't go at all well with his snazzy cape and his patent leather thigh-length riding boots.

A moment later they were joined by their three daughters and Vladimir, who was still clutching the silver micro-scooter. As the assembled vampires fell silent, Bruno tapped the microphone and said, 'One, two, three testing. One, two, three, testing.'

'One, two, three, testing. One, two, three testing,' replied the nine hundred vampires.

'No, *not* you!' yelled Bruno. 'That was just for the microphone!'

'Sorry, Ubervampire Blodvat,' said all the vampires.

'We forgive you,' said Hildegard. 'But only this once.'

'Good evilling, vampire hordes!' said Bruno. 'You are knowing why we are here.'

'Good evilling, Ubervampire Blodvat,' roared the nine hundred vampires. 'Yessss!

We serpently do know why we are here!'

'We are here for the coming back of the Master!'

'And we are here for the launch of the new Blodfurter, brought to you by Blodprods TM of Tonsilveinia, made with pure Perishable juice AB-negative!' cried Hildegard. 'Have you all got your free sample Blodfurters?'

'Yes, ve have!' roared the vampires, and they all waved their tiny sausages at her.

'Goooood!' yelled Hildegard. 'Soon you vill be nibbling them. And later, if you are very good and promise to buy lots and lots more Blodfurters, we are going to put one or two clapped out AB-minus Perishables in the gnawing ring so that you can all chase them around then bite them to drippy pieces!'

'But now,' said Bruno, 'it is time to bring back the Master! Do you know what date it is being?'

'Err – the forty-third of Septober?' suggested one rather dozy-looking vampire in the front row.

'The umpteenth of Febvember?' said his equally dim-looking friend.

'No!' said Bruno. 'It is being the sixth of November! A hundred years ago today some

104

wicked Perishables did stick their knives in the Master and make him go to dust. And then they brought him to Englandland and hid him in a secret place. But after much low and high searchings Madam Blodvat and myself have found the dusts.'

He clapped his hands twice and Mr Pither stepped forward wearing an awful porter's uniform which the Blodvats had obviously pinched from a hotel.

On the tray was a big jar of red liquid, which Claire knew was her grandpa's blood. Next to that was a metal box, which Claire knew was the Masons' best biscuit tin. Mr Pither set the tray on the altar in front of Bruno and withdrew. Then, with great ceremony, and much eyebrow-waggling, Bruno lifted up the biscuit tin full of vacuum cleaner dust so that the vampires could all see it, then cried, 'Here is the Master!'

'Hurrah!' yelled all the vampires.

Bruno lifted up the jar of blood and cried, 'And here is the blood of a Harker! A Harker who is now one of us! Ha ha ha!'

'Hurrah!' cried all the vampires.

Then, as the giant vampire once more began to wallop his corrugated iron, Bruno took the lid off the biscuit tin, unscrewed the top from the jar, and began to dribble the blood on to the dust while everyone watched with bated breath.

The jar was now almost empty. Bruno gave it a final shake and the very last drop of blood dripped on to the dust. As it did, there was an enormous explosion and a second later Bruno, Hildegard, their children and the altar all disappeared in a huge cloud of smoke while the black coach horses that had been standing quite placidly suddenly reared and screamed then galloped off out of the arena, dragging the coach after them and unceremoniously dumping the three vampire coachmen in a heap on the ground.

Seconds later, sparks, flashes and dazzling exploding stars began cascading from the spot where the biscuit tin had been. They were closely followed by six or seven more explosions, all equally spectacular, then by huge clouds of pink, blue and yellow smoke that rapidly enveloped the whole of the stage.

Claire was gobsmacked. 'Wow! That was pretty amazing! What's going on?'

'Just a little performance my special effects boys dreamed up,' muttered Professor Weatherwax. 'We've been so busy trying to extricate ourselves from the clutches of Sir Norman Goreman and his vampirized underlings that we missed last night's Guy Fawkes celebrations. So we thought we owed ourselves a little treat.'

As the smoke began to clear, Claire became aware of a small figure crouched on the altar where the biscuit tin had stood. It was hunched and sinister-looking and was still wreathed in swaithes of multicoloured smoke. As the smoke thinned, the figure slowly began to rise. When it was standing at its full height it opened its mouth to reveal the most enormous fangs Claire had ever seen on a vampire. It then opened its cape to reveal a rather tatty blue and beige tanktop which she recognized immediately. As it quickly closed the cape again, Bruno held up his hands, and in a voice that could have broken the church windows in Whitby, he bellowed, 'HE IS RETURNED!'

Nine hundred vampires all gasped as one, then fell to their knees in front of the ten-year-old Chumley school boy known as Darren Dobbs, then they all roared, 'Thanks be to Beelzebub! The Prince of Darkness has returned!'

'And all thanking to me also!' roared Bruno. Then he pointed to Hildegard and said, 'And to her!' Then he got a face full of smoke and began choking.

'It is he!' screamed Hildegard. 'We have brought him to you. Not to be mentioning the exciting new tasting sensation we are calling the Blodfurter! On sale soon at a crypt near you!'

'Yes!' cried Darren, as he stepped up to the microphone and flexed his shoulders. 'It is

I, Count Dracula! I am returned!' Then he quickly added, 'So you lot had better watch it.'

Once more, nine hundred vampires roared as one. 'We will, O Great One!'

Darren said, 'Right, that's that sorted, then!' He flapped his giant cape in what he obviously considered to be an heroically evil sort of way and twirled around.

As the vampires continued to whimper and grovel, Hildegard leaned across to Darren, coughed nervously, and said, 'Excuse me, Your Wickedness. I hope you are not minding me saying this, but you are looking much younger than I was thinking you would be.'

Darren said, 'Yes, it's the long rest. It did me the world of good. And that blood you tipped on me. It sort of refreshed me!'

Now recovered from his choking fit, Bruno bowed humbly to Count Dracula, then, said, 'Master, we had a great gift for you. A magnificent coach and horses. But they did run away. So perhaps you will be accepting something else in its place. Then he nodded to Vladimir who stepped forward and handed the Count the silver micro-scooter.

'Ah, wicked!' gasped Count Darren, enthusiastically accepting the scooter from

Vladimir and getting on it with the intention of doing a couple of celebratory laps of the stage.

But at that moment Bruno suddenly whipped out his giant Blodfurter and waved it at all the kneeling vampires, crying, 'Soon we will all bite a toast to the Master. Have your sausages ready! But before we do, the Master will be wanting to make a speech.'

'Will I?' said Darren.

'Yes! Yes!' yelled the vampires. 'Speech! Speech!' They began jumping up and down and thrusting their sausages into the air.

'All right,' said Count Darren. 'Here goes!' Then he cleared his throat and said, 'I can tell you, it wasn't much fun being a load of dust. But now I feel tons better! On this very day, the eighth of November, a hundred years ago, I was chased—'

'But your wickedness!' interrupted Hildegard. 'It was the sixth!'

''Course it was!' said Count Dracula. 'Whatever am I thinking of? On this very day the sixth of November, the evil Perishables stuck their dirty great knives into me. And believe me, it didn't half hurt! But now I'm as fit as a fiddle. I am ready to bite lots and lots of English Perishables. And then I will return to my castle in Siberia!'

'Your castle *where*?' said Hildegard, suddenly looking very alarmed.

'Oh dear,' whispered Professor Weatherwax.

'He never was any good at Geography,' muttered Claire.

'Siberia!' said Darren. 'It's where my castle is.'

'No, it's not!' said Hildegard.

'Where is it then?' said Darren.

'Not telling!' said Hildegard.

'Oh, go on!' said Darren.

'Shan't!' said Hildegard, looking at Darren with great suspicion.

But at that moment, Bruno suddenly waved his Blodfurter at the massed vampires and yelled, 'Long may the Master stay undead! Bite your sausages!' and although Hildegard screamed, 'No! Do not bite your sausages!' his thunderous roar drowned out her high-pitched screech and over eight hundred hungry bloodsuckers sank their teeth into the dodgy Blodfurters.

Three seconds later the reactions set in. Some vampires stood very still while great torrents of multi-coloured foam began to squirt from their mouths, ears and noses.

Soon they were knee deep in rainbow-coloured froth. Others went rigid, then began to lean in various directions at precisely forty-five degrees to the ground, and remain exactly like that. Professor Weatherwax experimentally reached out and gave one of these 'leaning' vampires a gentle push. It immediately crashed to the ground, then shattered into a thousand shivering pieces.

Meanwhile, dozens of other vampires had begun to swell to five times their normal size, until they exploded with an enormous BANG.

Otto's end was rather more spectacular. Rather than simply exploding, he floated several metres into the air, yelled something unpleasant in Tonsilveinian, quivered all over, then, to the accompaniment of some extremely rude noises, began to spin and whirl quite madly, like a balloon when the air's suddenly let out. After which he exploded with a bang that could probably have been heard in Chumley.

As Otto's nose and ears landed at his feet, Professor Weatherwax turned to Claire and said, 'This mixture of AB-negative blood and Safebury's Mediterranean garlic and herb really is quite lethal! Remind your grandfather to let me have the recipe some time.'

While all this mayhem was going on around Claire and the Professor, more chaos was happening on stage. Bruno was not only choking but swelling and going extremely floppy, as if his bones were turning to rubber. He desperately looked for someone to help him, only to see that his four children had now fled the stage, totally freaked by the huge and terrifying-looking squad of Extreme Exterminators who were now charging down the hillside opposite. He turned to Hildegard, but she was otherwise engaged, trying to

throttle Darren, furiously swinging the poor
lad from side to side like the pendulum of
some huge living clock. If Grandpa Reg hadn't
suddenly appeared on the stage and grabbed
Bruno's discarded sausage, Darren might well
have been a goner. Holding the sausage like
cricket bat, Grandpa ran at Hildegard, then,
with all the power and fury of a man half his
age, gave her an almighty wallop on the back of
the head. It sent her sprawling, causing her to
release Darren, who leapt away.

'Come on then, Fig Face!' growled
Grandpa Reg. 'Do you want some more?'

Hildegard *did* want some more! Revealing
a set of fangs that would have put a great

white shark to shame, she charged. Grandpa Reg's timing was perfect. He held his nerve until Hildegard was almost upon him, and he let fly with a wallop that any Test cricketer would have been proud of!

The blood pudding caught Hildegard straight between her teeth. Her fearsome fangs clamped shut on the power-packed pudding. Grandpa Reg wrenched the sausage from Hildegard's jaws, leaving her holding a great chunk between her teeth. Then he clobbered her again. The shock of the blow to her tum caused her to give an almighty gulp and swallow the fatal chunk of pudding. She immediately stuck her hand down her own throat and began frantically fishing around for the sausage with those horrendous talon-like nails. Unfortunately, her fishing wasn't precise. After a second, she did manage to pull something out. But it definitely wasn't the sausage. It was a piece of her own windpipe!

Determined not to be beaten, she plunged her hand in again. This time she pulled out what looked like a rib. Then over and over again, frenziedly pulling out all sorts of bits and pieces, many of which belonged to her most vital organs. Of course, ripping your own insides to shreds isn't the sort of thing you can do indefinitely, especially when one of the vital bits and pieces you grab happens to be your own heart. It was when Hildegard seized this particular organ that things came to a swift and sudden end. She let out a long scream, her eyes rolled back in their sockets and she collapsed to the floor, twitched a few times, and that was that. Horrible Hildegard Blodvat was no more.

Bruno crawled towards her and groaned, 'My dear, I am coming!' Due to his swiftly swelling body and his rapidly rubberizing bones he now resembled a cross between an overweight walrus and a giant beach ball. He'd also become extremely bouncy. So when Mr Pither ran across the stage and planted a huge kick on his blubbery bottom, he flew into the air then *bdoinggged* wildly around the stage before finally sailing over the edge and landing on the upturned face of a vanquished vampire. As luck would have it, the vampire's mouth was wide open so its fangs immediately pierced Bruno's flabby bottom, causing him to explode about four times more violently than Otto had done.

Bruno's bits and pieces landed amongst the

hundreds of doomed vampires that now littered the parade ground. Many of them had now succumbed to their unpleasant conditions and were lying around in various stages of decay and decomposition.

However, a hundred or so vampires who had been standing towards the back of the crowd and hadn't heard Bruno's command to bite their sausages were still more or less intact. Not for long though, because they were being systematically bombarded by Professor Weatherwax's camouflage-clad Extreme Exterminator forces who had miraculously appeared out of the woods the moment the vamps had bitten their puds. They were busily hurling pineapple-shaped missiles into the midst of surviving vampires. As one of these exploded amongst the Undead, throwing several of them two or three metres into the air, Claire turned to Professor Weatherwax and said, 'What are they?'

'Garlic grenades!' said the Professor. 'Very effective, don't you think?'

Suddenly several high-pitched screams rang out at the far side of the parade ground and by the beams of the huge flashlights the Professor's people had trained on the vamp camp, Claire was able to see the three Blodvat sisters leaping and dodging their way through the heaps of twitching vampire bodies, their hair and skirts flying, as they attempted to make their escape.

Just when it looked like they might reach the top, two girls on ponies came galloping over the ridge, not only cutting off their escape route but effectively driving them back down again. As the Blodvat sisters reeled this way and that, Poppy and Rose handled their ponies like the most expert pair of cowgirls ever to come out of the Wild West.

They wheeled and chased and harried, never once giving the vampire girls the chance to attempt a lucky lift-off. The Mason twins deliberately began to manoeuvre the Blodvat sisters towards a small group of trees. At the moment they reached the trees, a net dropped from the lower branches, ensnaring them entirely and leaving them struggling like three trapped tigresses.

A moment later, Jason and Sandy climbed down from the trees and joined the Mason twins to watch the rather gruesome final moments of the doomed sisters. Then, as the four Vigilantes stared in horrified fascination at

the twitching, frothing, foaming sisters, something large and glittery flashed past them.

It was Vladimir! Because of his aversion to blood he hadn't bitten into his sausage and was now taking advantage of his excellent health and the micro-scooter to make his escape. In just a few more seconds he had reached the ridge. Then, with one almighty last power-packed thrust he scooted himself right off the edge of the ridge, threw out his arms, flapped them a couple of times, and was airborne! A moment later, he was gone!

Chapter Nine
Vigilantes Victorious

Ten minutes after that, the battle of the Devil's Wash Basin was over.

'Right, I think that more or less wraps things things up!' said Professor Weatherwax, as his Exterminators dragged the last of the vanquished vamps into the huge lorries that Jason's dad had so kindly provided for their disposal. 'Rather messy, but a most satisfactory result! How are you Darren? Have my medical staff sorted you out?'

'Not bad thanks,' said Darren. 'But my throat still hurts a bit.'

'That Hildegard always was a pain in the neck!' said Grandpa Reg.

'I must say, you made a fine young Dracula!' the Professor said to Darren.

'That was really something!' said Claire. 'How did you set that up?'

'After my bit of trouble with Sir Norman and his pals I finally got back to my office and found your e-mails waiting for me,' said Professor Weatherwax. 'Having assessed the situation, I contacted Jason and Darren, then it was simply a matter of getting myself and my team to the Eck Valley. Helicopters are excellent in an emergency. Then I remembered my idea about providing the Blodvats with a "Master". I was thinking of using my own chap but then this young fellow volunteered. We needed someone small and nimble so my disguise bods got to work. After that a couple of my best undercover people posed as vamps and smuggled him in.'

'But where were you before the explosions, Darren?' said Claire.

'In that Welcome Back Drac coffin!' said Darren. 'When I heard the bangs I jumped out and got myself on the altar!'

'Pity about your Geography, though!' said the Professor.

'I blame the teachers!' said Mr Pither.

'Well at least the vamps bit their spiked sausages!' said the Professor. 'That was a tremendous idea of yours, Claire. And the results were quite astounding!'

'We've got to thank Grandpa Reg for that!' said Claire. 'He did the mixing.'

'Well, you know what they say,' said Grandpa Reg. 'The proof of the pudding is in the eating.'

'So is that it then?' said Sandy. 'Are all the vamps wiped out?'

'Ah!' said Professor Weatherwax. 'I wish I could say that. But I doubt it! We've definitely struck a massive blow against the Undead. But by no means are they vanquished. No doubt there are more where they came from. And to be honest with you, I don't even feel entirely certain we've seen the last of the Blodvats.'

'Really?' said Poppy.

'Yes,' said Professor Weatherwax. 'One can be never be entirely sure of anything where the Undead are concerned. They have a habit of popping up again, just when you think you've seen the last of them. One must always be vigilant!'

'Or even a Vampire Vigilante!' said Claire.

'But what about Vladimir?' said Rose. 'We don't know what happened to him!'

'Young Vladimir is the least of my worries,' said the Professor. 'The Undead are supposed to be the embodiment of evil but I don't think that applies in his case. I'm certainly not going to be pursuing him too energetically.'

At that moment one of the Professor's assistants appeared at his side and said, 'We've had the medical team check the hostages and none of them seem to be too bad. They're all ready and waiting now.'

'OK, Vigilantes!' said the Professor. 'Before we all go our separate ways I want to say a word or two to everyone here. So, if you'll just follow me up on to the stage.'

The hordes of vampires had been replaced by the captives in the Blood Shed. All of them were smiling up at them and looking extremely happy to be free again. Even Dr Grainger seemed his cheerful old self again, despite his ordeal with the leeches.

The Professor walked up to the microphone then said, 'Thank you all for waiting around. I realize that after what you have been through you will be wanting to get back to your homes and families. But before my people ferry you to your various destinations, there are a few things I want to say. First of all I must ask you not to breathe a word about what you have seen this evening

123

and during the past few days and weeks. I realize this will be hard for some of you, but it is vital! You will all be provided with suitable alibis for your absences from home. The fight against the forces of darkness goes on and for reasons of efficiency and security it is essential that knowledge of these events does not reach the general public. And of course all of you will receive compensation for your terrible ordeal. There is a secret government fund available that entitles you all to several thousand pounds in cash.'

A murmur of approval ran through the people and several of them nodded.

'But now, I come to the most important thing I want to say,' continued Professor Weatherwax. 'I'd like to introduce you to six very remarkable young people. Without them I don't think you would be standing there listening to me now. We all have a lot to thank them for. It is because of their courage, staying power and intelligence that the forces of evil have been so soundly beaten. On your behalf and mine I'd like to say an absolutely massive "Thank you".' Then he gestured towards the six children and said, 'I give you the Vampire Vigilantes!' And with that the people began clapping and cheering as if they'd never stop.

The cheers of the rescued people were still ringing in Claire's ears half an hour later when she and Grandpa Reg walked into the living room of 24, Whitby Gardens.

'Where have you two been?' said her mum. 'We were beginning to get very worried! I realize you left that note, but it really is late. You know Grandpa Reg, I'm beginning to think I preferred it when you moped around in bed all day. At least I knew where you were!'

'Mum's right to be worried,' said Mr Whimsy. 'Since that awful business with Dr Grainger and Mr Legg, everyone in Chumley's been wondering what the next bad news will be!'

'It's all right, Dad,' said Claire. 'Everyone can stop worrying now. Dr Grainger and Mr Legg have been found and they're OK. We got the good news not long ago!'

'Oh, that's wonderful!' said Mum. 'So where were they then?'

'They'd sort of got err, carried away,' said

125

Grandpa Reg. 'On Hallowe'en night! We don't know the details. But I'm sure we'll find out sooner or later.'

'But what about you two?' said Dad. 'Where've *you* been?'

'We've been with Bruno and Hildegard,' said Grandpa Reg.

'Oh, that will have been nice. So how are they?' said Dad.

'Well, actually,' said Claire, 'when we left them, they weren't looking too good.'

'That's right!' said Grandpa Reg. 'I think it must have been something they ate.'

'I think they might even have decided to call it a day,' said Claire.

'What?' said Mum 'Do you mean go back to Tonsilveinia?'

'Something like that,' said Grandpa Reg. 'I think they got homesick.'

'Does that mean we won't be seeing them again?' said Dad.

'Looks like it,' Grandpa Reg replied.

'Aah, what a pity!' sighed Mum. 'I'd loved to have said goodbye to them. Then again, perhaps they're missing those lovely children of theirs so much that they can't stay a moment longer. It is a shame though. They were such a nice couple!'

'Yes,' said Mr Whimsy. 'Really nice. And so sophisticated.'

Despite the fact that she was exhausted, Claire couldn't get to sleep. She kept turning the amazing events of the day over and over in her mind. And after that she began thinking about tomorrow. All of a sudden she'd realized that from now on life was probably going to feel very empty. It was rather an odd thought, but she did wonder if she might get a bit bored with life, now that there was no longer anything to fear or battle against.

With this thought in mind she began to drift off to sleep. She couldn't have dozed off for more than a couple of minutes when she heard the gentlest toot of a car horn in the street outside. She got out of bed then went to her window and opened the curtain just a crack.

Parked directly opposite her house was a huge Mercedes estate car. As she watched, the car's doors opened and six figures got out. As

Claire stared in utter disbelief and amazement, Bruno and Hildegard Blodvat and their four children looked up at her window and waved. Thinking she was imagining things, Claire turned to look at Wendy. If this was the Blodvats he'd certainly be up and growling. But he wasn't, he was still fast asleep. So she turned back to check the scene outside for a second time. But the car and the Blodvats were gone.

THE END